THAT WE MIGHT NEVER MEET AGAIN

PHIL ROBINSON

That We Might Never
Meet Again

faber and faber

To James, for the challenge

First published in 2005
by Faber and Faber Limited
3 Queen Square London WC1N 3AU

Printed in England by Mackays of Chatham, plc

A CIP record for this book
is available from the British Library

ISBN 0–571–22550–0

2 4 6 8 10 9 7 5 3 1

Prologue

Dear Anna,

You asked about killing. I wasn't sure if you meant vermin or game. Naturally, we kill both.

Each year we have some squirrels to trap, greys which migrate in. We have reds here and we try to preserve that population. We live-trap so that any reds caught can be released again. The greys are dispatched with a blow to the head. It's not difficult. You put a hessian sack over the opening of the trap and angle the trap upwards, so that the opening is up, that is. The squirrel runs up to escape, the same instinct as tree climbing when threatened, I would guess. It will push as far into the sack as it can, which usually means a corner. When it's done you have just a still, warm body. When the life is gone there is nothing and it's amazing how easily the life can be extinguished, as if their grip on the world is tenuous. I leave the bodies under the nearest bush. Jim takes them for the pot, Simon feeds them to his ferrets. The rear legs and saddle are good but too fiddly for me. I check the traps on the way to the gardens and those within the garden itself. Simon and Jim see to those in the demesne.

The deer are both vermin and game. Vermin because of the damage they do to the trees, the young ones in particular. Sorry, I'm not being clear tonight, the young trees. Game because people will pay handsomely to come and shoot them. Mostly it's folk from London but we do draw regulars from places like Holland, Denmark, and the States are of course a big market. The Yanks will pay to shoot anything. His lordship takes a few and that does for a typical breeding year, though, if numbers are very high then we might need to cull. Most of the meat goes up to the house, obviously, but some does get divvied up. Generally it is just hung but Jack always smokes a bit, which takes the edge off the richness. He has a special recipe with the chips, one for deer, another for salmon, yet another for the different birds. He's the estate carpenter, I think I've mentioned him before – the one with eyes of different colours.

Simon does raise some birds, partridge mostly. Again, his lordship takes some and the rest are for shoots. Corporate stuff or lawyers. Ask around, you might know somebody who has been up. It's not real shooting, more like slaughter. City types don't tend to be the greatest shots unless they're ex-army. They wing as many as they kill cleanly and then it's up to us to pick up and dispatch. The 'guests' get a brace each to take away, which will probably be the most expensive thing they eat in a year. We usually all get a brace as an extra for helping, not that we have a choice or even would wish to have. It is part of the life here and the income from it is truly staggering. Strange, though, to have people here for so short a time and for such a reason. I sometimes wonder what they think about on the way home, whether the place touches them at all. They always seem so solid in their groups, braying, almost as if overcompensating.

The proper shooting his lordship keeps for himself and his friends. There is excellent wildfowl about the place. Ducks of course, but snipe, woodcock, and quail as well. Native quail, mind. It was reintroduced but has done just fine. It is better that it is just a select group who shoot these. The numbers are more easily controlled and the kills are cleaner.

Rabbits are a free-for-all and everybody here, pretty much, shoots them whenever. Even so we still have to cull every so often. The dogs get mine mostly, which is fair as it is usually they that catch them. There wouldn't be a week go by without them eating rabbit. I might bother once or twice a month but to be honest, I'm not that keen. I prefer pigeon and I've always got the chickens here if I fancy some white meat.

Hares are sacred. It has been the way here for a long time. I rein the dogs in when I see them. They are truly beautiful.

Why did you ask? Have you had one of the cats put down?

We're enjoying an Indian summer at the moment. It means more grass cutting, which is a bind, but the late raspberries are still fruiting whereas last year they'd stopped by two weeks past.

I must admit it's been a quiet sort of month and I don't have much news. Sally is showing signs of arthritis in her left shoulder and is a bit stiff in the mornings first thing. I don't want to bring her in just yet. None of us is getting any younger it seems.

Some artist is supposed to be coming to paint soon. He is young, which I guess means cheap, and I think he was at the Academy so he shouldn't be too bad. I don't know his name – I've heard nothing but gossip so far – so I'm not getting too excited. All will be revealed in due course, no doubt. It will provide a passing interest whilst he is here – another reminder of the world beyond the hills.

I hope you are keeping well. Regards to Patrick.

Love, as ever,
S

It was not winter. Overnight the wind had blown from the north, clearing away the cloud and leaving the stars to shine brightly treacherous. By morning it had left a portent of the change in the seasons. He knew it as he lay in bed, even before he opened his eyes. He realised now that he had known it in the night as the air cooled and the chill had seeped into his dreams. The air which flowed through the open window carried death.

He had slept with open windows most of his life. He loved the feel of the temperature changes and the scents peculiar to the night. In one of his childhood homes there had been a large jasmine which grew right up to the window of his parents' bedroom, and in summer when the window was left open almost permanently, the tendrils would explore inwards, twisting around themselves for support. It was not much to look at even in flower. The small white stars were hidden amongst the dark green of the foliage. But on sunny days in June, the scent would build and from the early evening, as the day cooled, it would be carried through the air to the terrace below and fill their room with the dreams of renaissance lovers. He knew now as he had not known then, that such delicacies would not have been lost on his parents even if the over developed sense of guilt of born-damned Calvinists totally disguised any outward display of carnal affection. Pleasures were hidden as the star flowers were hidden and there was no honesty in that place. Not that he wasted any conscious thought on it, although still at night sometimes he would be at 'home', if home is where the parents are, and it would be there. It disturbed him like little else. It was now half a lifetime since he had been there; half a lifetime of many changes. In that house the windows had been large wooden casements, ill maintained and easily provoked by the slightest wind despite their heaviness. To sleep in the breeze there involved wedges of folded paper and emergency blankets, as that house with its high ceilings and blackened stone would haemorrhage heat like no other. The windows here were casements too, the houses were a similar age, but they fitted snugly and were altogether more delicate. The scale helped no doubt, this being just a cottage and there was no sense of the carpenter having to work beyond himself.

Summer nights that brought rain were his favourites. First there would be that smell, a damp mustiness as if the earth itself was opening its skin in anticipation of the blessing to be bestowed. Then would come the sudden drop in temperature as the air sighed with relief. A sigh of one who has been stooped under the weight of a heavy burden as it swings from his shoulders. And the rain itself; sudden fat drops which would splatter the window as they fell lazily or the drumming on the roof like the voice of Jeremiah with wind-driven urgency. At these times he would slide between waking and sleeping, from solitude to the arms of a dark angel who had loved him perhaps, despite everything.

He squeezed his eyes tight, forcing the blood from the lids and turning them dark. The dahlias in the double border would blacken as the day wore on, their frost-fractured cells succumbing to the heat from the sun in a clear sky. He considered not getting up, resenting as always the obligation. Thoughts of weekends and university filled his mind, when to get up was a joy, as the time was his own. He relaxed and the blood returned, back-lit red. He watched his breath furl out a few times before emitting a sound which was both a sigh and a groan; a resolution to face the day. His naked skin rose in goose bumps as he crossed the room, his sack tightening against his body. He opened the wooden shutters fully and blinked against the greater light. It would be a bastard, he decided, no two ways about it. His jeans were cold from

2

the night when he retrieved them from the chair and he pulled them on before heading down to the kitchen where a shirt would be toasting on the towel rail of the range. As he passed the back door he flipped the latch, unleashing a surge of hounds who woofled and wagged with the ecstasy of reunion. He ignored them.

He lifted the round, slip-glazed pot of porridge from the slow oven and set it atop to cool slightly. The espresso pot came next, which he primed with its shot of bitter coffee, pressing down the charge with the side of his thumb, his body remembering the movements and not requiring his consciousness, which was as well as it was away and somewhere else. The guttering of the pot would be his signal to engage and he poured the steaming liquor into the cup already prepared with a spoon of creeping demerara. His tongue stained black from the first sip, he could now roll the cigarette from the pouch he kept at the side of the oven. Thus armed he concluded a ritual which had characterised his life for the last ten years, ever since he arrived on the estate. It was a long time since he had thought of changing it. Indeed it was the very lack of thought which was the ritual's appeal. It soothed and comforted his soul into the day. The cyclical repetition disguised the time-scale, disguised his failure to act decisively, although in the brief moments of introspection he knew the only reason not to act was apathy.

He turned at last to the dogs, greeting each in turn according to the pack order they had established between themselves. No use working against their understanding of the world, he had concluded. He set down the bowls prepared the night before and retired to the table. Sat against it with his right elbow resting thereon, he could service alternately his needs for the cigarette and the coffee whilst his left hand toyed casually with the velvet ear of an already finished Sally. He rolled it between thumb and forefinger, feeling the ridges of cartilage and the yielding skin. He wondered how dogs could find this comforting, but he had known it instinctively

3

as a child, just as he had known that if a dog's nose is touched it will lick to clean it and so, as a toddler he would solicit these affections and fearlessly pursue even the largest dogs until he could squeeze their noses between forefinger and thumb, much to the surprise of the owners. Such displays of dominance no doubt preserved him from the bites he deserved.

The stupidity of the day hit him for a second time. Today would bring 'weekly business' up at the house. His lordship seemed decidedly settled for this time of year and showed no signs of fleeing south as he normally did. A frost might strengthen his resolve and that would be a compensation at least. Weekly business was a recent innovation to 'facilitate the easy running of the estate'. Or similar bollocks. His mind numbed at the prospect. The cast remained the same; the work followed the cycle of the seasons. And yet, and yet there must be so many words, and so many of the same words at that. Perhaps repeating the lines preserved the status quo, or reassured the players that the game was indeed entertaining, like a novice at the bridge table who will say, 'My, this is fun,' a million times on the first evening and half a million times on the second until, by the third evening, probably within the same week, is craving the monotony of the shuffle and the deal, and the strain of polite conversation. And how it could take the best half of a morning when there was work to be done, he would never know. It was all so unexpected; this innovation had, at first, seemed like some brainstorm on the part of Lord Palmer. But people had gone mad for it, as if their years of silently getting on with it had been a mycelium growing away beneath the leaf litter, penetrating the roots. Now, in the damp of autumn it was time to mushroom and spore. He never thought he could have misjudged so many people. The only hope now was for the fungus to be merely parasitic and not fatal; a last vestige of their previous lives which would exhaust itself and die.

He pressed the life out of his cigarette against the tarnished silver of a finely crafted ashtray. He ate his porridge directly

4

from the pot with little pleasure; it was a duty he owed to his body if he were to demand of it work. It was a duty he owed his staff; gardening on an empty stomach shortens the temper.

* * *

The walk across the park could not fail to lift the spirits of even the most jaded. In the distance, the long, low line of the hills glistened in the autumnal early sun. Like a recumbent sleeping giant the hills rose in unequal steps at each end, sweeping up from the feet to the waist and from there to the shoulder in a progressively steeper ridge which would tire the legs of even the sternest walker. At the head, the climb was nearly vertical and doubly daunting because, when engaged on the first stretch, the prospect of the rise past the collarbone to the shoulder itself remained unseen. Each must be a thousand feet, and of the few climbers who attempted it each year some fell to their deaths. Some would have informed the authorities of their plans, so when they failed to reappear a helicopter would be sent and would drone lazily, sometimes landing, sometimes flying away fruitlessly. Others would not have planned for such an outcome. If it was early in the season they would probably be found by subsequent parties. Those who succumbed late in the season would spend the winter on the slopes and would provide a welcome meal for the corbies and gulls and anything else with the strength or guile to reach whatever jutting ledges had brought the poor unfortunates' last journey to an end. Climbers returning home from their holidays would praise the difficulty of the rock and the magnificence of the scenery and here, in this photo, is a bird's nest. Look at the brightly coloured material the bird has found to mix with the heather twigs and the plastic washed up on the shore to the north. The forgotten colours of last year's fashions. Their ignorance was for the best perhaps, as now they would keep returning until, one day, when their knees are not what they were, and their judgement is dulled by repeated success, they too will

5

succumb to the caress of what the locals called, when there were still locals, 'the endless dreamer'. What the giant dreamt of was not remembered, nor why he had slept for so long. Still, the timelessness of those dreams were the comfort for the community of the estate which nestled beneath his sheltering hulk.

He knew that the hill demanded vision. The hill was life itself. On its flank it seduced the spirit of the sky, coaxing the rain to fill the many streams which tumbled from the heights into the lough below, peat-stained and vibrant with brown trout; an ever-flowing presence. With its head it turned the wind, sheltering the trees on its lee, which brought forth berries in gratitude, feeding the birds through the cold of winter. It carried the seasons on its shoulders and returned the blessing of the sun in ever-changing colour. At night its shadow defined the stars, binding their limits on the horizon, legislating their terms of rising and setting. Its colours formed the music of the dreams of the sleepers who, each in their beds alone, wandered among the birch wood of the lower slopes in spring and swam in the waters of the lough in summer. The hill was life itself. This understanding came with submission and time. His mind was rambling and he tried to shrug it off; his gods were the gods of the high places, he had decided many years before, and when the time came he had returned to this faith.

His speculation ended with the empty sky before him. He ran the last stretch to the brow of the drumlin that bounded Sun's Rest, the dogs cavorting at this new game. A leaden dullness crept into his heaving chest as breathlessly he took it in. He had seen it happen once before towards the end of a long, dry summer. Heavy rain had soaked the ground and the oak had drunk heavily. The sudden expansion of cells too much, their increased weight too heavy for the tree to bear in its weakened state. The wound then had bled water for days. If he had been able to cry the tears would have rolled but his eyes just ached dryly, unblinking at the mess that was the

6

great oak. The tree was wrenched apart, the flesh of its trunk split and laid bare, a rupture of pale jaggedness which broke through what remained of the canopy. The branch tips had shattered into matches as the uppermost bough had answered the call of the hard dry earth. Its beauty was gone for ever.

The estate was buzzing with talk of the artist and his wife who had arrived the previous night, or in truth, early morning, and who had knocked the entire house up in their efforts to find a bed. They, like many before, had got lost on the road. The road itself was fine. Like a labyrinth there was only one way, so the possibilities for getting lost were nil. But, like a labyrinth, it tested the commitment of those who travelled. Their conviction must have wavered as the unlikely prospect of finding a dwelling, let alone an entire estate, had proved too much of a stumbling block. In his mind they had failed the first test of faith in Inchnamactaire, but his curiosity was still pricked right enough, primed as it had been by Lady Palmer's words from the day before: *oblige* was such an ambiguous request.

The grapes could not be delayed longer, not if it was going to freeze overnight for the rest of the week, as it seemed determined to do. Too much work had been invested to allow them to spoil now. He took Ben, the youngest of the garden staff and the least demanding, and set off to the vinery. Jim and Adam he had sent out with the saws to brash up the oak boughs and dress the tree if need be. Jack had looked it over the day before and marked the usable pieces into lengths with chalk, precious little in all. The rest would be stacked in the yard for firewood for the year after next. Oak is a slow drier and far too heavy when wet to be messing around with more than necessary.

The lads had been as high as kites and some good heavy work would help calm them, he thought, if they didn't have an accident first. The discipline of marrying Lucy to a cart should have forestalled them enough. Lucy, a difficult gelding who never seemed to have forgiven his masters for his castration and who seemed to sense the indignity of the feminine abbreviation. An unguarded hand or a careless manner was likely to be rewarded with a nip or a turn into the sheugh by the drive. This risk meant that people did the job with more care than they might have done otherwise and he knew that Lucy would see them out safely and back again. Besides, his ego could cope with the muffled 'twat' as the lads left the bothy.

Ben was dispatched to check the fruit store, which would be fine as it was always just fine. He needed some moments to himself, though, to walk across the garden slowly, to observe the results of yesterday's emergency tidying operation – Lady Palmer did so hate to see all the dead flowers – to think of nothing in particular. He stopped at the dipping pool and rolled a cigarette. The water still and gelid from the night before. An early bumblebee had fallen on to the surface and described circles, the wings uppermost powering it unevenly. It stopped its futile beating and drifted whilst it re-amassed its strength before trying again. He realised he was numb. The things that had always consoled him had begun to wear thin. He could not even stir himself to break the surface of the water with the bamboo cane he seemed to have acquired from somewhere. He raised his head, sighing and exhaling a plume of smoke, visible then invisible. He stared at the brick of the garden wall, pock-marked by the penetration of so many nails over the years, allowing his eyes to slip out of focus, filling his vision with the patterned red. He shook his head back to the present and dismissed it as the change in the seasons. He always suffered in spring and autumn. The changes made him dissatisfied with the remnants of the world he enjoyed. The dogs still helped but at times even their dependence held him only weakly. He roused to his name being called and Ben's hurried steps on the gravel. His brow flickered annoyance, which gave Ben pause.

'I forgot to ask, do you want the bottles filling?'

'I forgot to tell you. No, don't worry for it, wait till the water warms up a touch. Just check we've enough bottles.'

Ben was gone with a smile. A good lad, a little timid around himself perhaps but fine with the others and that was enough.

The vine house was a wonder of Victorian manufacture and transport; a ridiculous extravagance then, in the days of cheap fuel and labour, and much more so now. An extravagance on which Lord Palmer insisted, however, terrified as he was of contamination by genetically modified anything. Besides, 'What's the point of all this if one cannot have grapes' and 'Vitis – the plant of life, you know'. He loved Lord Palmer at those times. So grapes were grown and the season had been good, particularly for the muscats. He tried to think through what conditions may have favoured them so especially this year but couldn't place anything immediately. He would talk it through with the lads; they might have ideas. The days just seemed to slip past him now, his sense of time withered by neglect.

The house took up the full south-facing wall of the fruit garden, well in excess of two hundred feet. It had been shipped from Glasgow in sections with a team of workmen to install it, some of whom had not returned home. He still marvelled at the care with which every detail had been designed. The ironwork was finely rounded and pleasing to the eye. The terminal finials rose in palm fronds, each frondlet textured and differentiated even though few would ever see them, twenty feet above the ground as they were. The glass, which had arrived in one hundred straw-packed cases – more than was needed so that repairs would be easy to make – was scalloped across the plane so that the water ran down the centres away from the vulnerable framework. A framework still as sound as the day it was installed, though it was the devil's own job to paint it every third year. The vents still rose easily and silently on their screws. The slope of the roof perfect to catch the light at this latitude, perfect to the eye. There had been pride and there had been care and the whole structure had still a satisfying fullness like the fullness of bitter chocolate in the mouth. A fullness only enhanced by the slight imperfections. Some of the panes had a greenish tinge, some pinkish, others more yellow, stained by the contaminant ores that must have been present in the different batches. Most were pure. On the clear days of winter, when the vines were bare, the light would dapple the fine pale stone of the paving inside. He would sit in the unseasonable warmth in this fecund cathedral and smoke through the silence.

The grapes were at the peak of their powers. The roots had sunk deeply into the raised soil beds on the outside of the house and were well into the clay. A liberal anointing with well-rotted manure preserved the structure of the soil and was faithfully rewarded by the harvests. The fruit though not large had an intense flavour, an oiliness almost, which coated the tongue. Vitis – the plant of life.

He worked quickly with Ben and they exchanged few words, as those who see each other every day cease to talk, especially when what is expected is so deeply understood. They snipped out the bunches with the stork-billed secateurs, checking each one for undeveloped, bruised or mouldy grapes, which they detached deftly into a bucket. Each bunch they laid on to flat baskets woven from soft grass which did not damage the fruit. One layer only, each bunch with its attendant length of stalk to insert into the bottle of sugar solution. The racked bottles allowed the bunches to hang in the air just as they did on the vine and delayed the progression into currants.

As they filled a basket they carried it through to the store, arranging the bunches by cultivar and inserting a paper label at the beginning and end of each row. Sometimes the cook would come down herself or even his lordship, and they would need to know which was which. There would be grapes on every table of the estate tonight, unwashed and covered in bloom. He knew the tastes of everybody and would make sure they had their favourite. Later on they could not be so choosy but this first picking was a tradition he had inherited and he was happy to observe it.

They had worked solidly for nearly two hours, stripping the vines and stripping themselves gradually as the sun climbed and made it uncomfortably warm under the glass, even at this time of year. The tea break was fast approaching and Ben was starting to get edgy, in thrall to his stomach at all times. Their visitor had been watching them for some while before she spoke, admiring the concentration of the work; the sustained dexterity. Her previous relationship had been with a ceramicist and she still found the manipulation of objects seductive. It was the fluidity of the movements, the body trained to the discipline of the craft, the unconscious action. And something more.

'Lady Palmer said that I would find the gardens "most diverting" despite the frost. Perhaps you would care to show me.'

He set down his secateurs, 'Of course. It would be a pleasure.'

'Would you like to try a grape?' Ben was desperate to be included. He watched as she smiled, advancing on the basket proffered by Ben; very knowing, he thought, and graceful. Slim fingers reached out and she nipped the plumpest grape of the bunch free with her delicately polished nails; another smile for Ben. Then those eyes of liquid jade turned on him for the first time, gazing upwards from under generous lashes. He remained impassive as she half pressed the grape against her front teeth and half bit down, the pale red juice bursting from the skin and filling her mouth before her lips ended the scene. One bead of juice escaped and glistened proudly. She seemed in no hurry to lick it away, enjoying the feel of it perhaps, or the effect it was having. He was flattered she thought

12

him worthy of these charms and, had he been younger, might have believed they could have been exclusive to him. He gathered up his shirt.

'Break time, Ben. Carry on here at ten, I'll come back when I can.'

* * *

The garden was a world within a world, where space was folded and compressed – dense layers of form and texture resonant with meaning; where space was stretched out, catching the unwary who, when confronted with a vista of sublime beauty, would have to be reminded to breathe, if the tightness of their chest would permit it. The planting was as dense as the land allowed, then broken with open spaces; spaces like bars of silence. And, like bars of silence, the absence seemed to signify more and to endure for longer in the memory. If the structure was a music that resided in the soul and the space silence, the plants themselves were a song of nuanced history, there to be explored and translated by those who were willing.

They started with the vegetables laid out each side of them, like the cohorts of an army. Stout leeks in their rows; cabbages and other brassicas for evermore. The air carried the sour taint of them, even this early in the day. The uncut ferns of the asparagus waved at him in accusation; when the grapes were finished, they would be next.

Her interest in these was slight; she had seen vegetables growing before and although she did not know it, she was blind to the possibility that it could be for anything other than a hobby – a supplement to food purchased. The seriousness with which this man treated them, though, as if they were the most important part of the garden, entertained her. She watched as his eyes followed the rows, making judgements all the while as to the quality of the produce.

He was starting to believe that this tour would be hard work when they arrived at the espaliers and cordons of top

fruit, trained to their wires. Generations of pruning had distorted their growth, forcing an unnatural fruitfulness which
hung now from the laterals and spurs, wet with the moisture
of the thaw. The regularity of these sculpted forms fascinated
her and he was happy to explain the process, returning to a
theme of time more than once in a way that made her smile.
As she listened she trailed a lazy finger through a dew-spotted
spider's web, the owner running out then retreating hastily to
the edge as the last of the tension was broken and the web
hung free in the breeze.

'Would you like to taste one?' He indicated the pears with
a nod.

'Please. That one!' she pronounced, placing a finger to a
plump one, its base reddened through exposure to the sun.

He twisted it free and halved it with a knife. He made to cut
again when she stopped him with a hand.

'Don't worry. I've got good teeth.' She smiled to prove it,
biting into her half, and laughing as the juice flowed down
her chin. 'It's still cold.'

He smiled at her and split his half again, returning the knife
to his pocket.

They continued on, stopping once to admire a pear which
rose to the height of the wall, its dark, fissured bark bare of
leaves.

'It was such a perfect form that we left it. But it's starting to
lose branches now,' he explained without waiting for her
question.

'I was wondering what they would be like in winter. Where
next?'

He led her out by the north gate at the rear of the vinery
and made at first towards the Hall along a broad grass path
which ran within a canyon formed by the unassailable, blackened stone of the garden wall on their left and a cemetery-
dark yew hedge, equal in height to the wall, on their right. He
sensed her irritation in the unquiet way she breathed, though
what the cause might be remained a mystery; he had thought

14

they were making progress.

'I came down this way; I've seen all this already.' The disputes of the night before were fighting for her attention and, for an hour or two, she wished to be free of her husband.

'This is the best way to begin the rest.' She would need to acquire patience, he thought, if she were to last any length of time here. 'Trust me.'

They relapsed into silence; he was enjoying the contrasting colours of the frost-yellowed morello leaves, fan-trained against the wall, and thinned out by the cold so that just a tracery remained. The fallen leaves lay in pools beneath each tree – the air had been still as they dropped – and that sweet smell with its sharp edge of decay which caught in the nose was starting to rise from them. So evocative of this time of year he thought, and so fleeting. Fleeting as the minute which may have passed before the intrusion of her frustration. It seemed to grow with every step as the east gable of the Hall loomed into view – so neatly framed by their surroundings, until it was too great to be ignored longer. He heard her breathing change beside him and he knew she was about to speak out again. Gently he touched her arm with his left hand, the fingers slightly spread and as straight as he could manage, forestalling her whilst his right hand gestured towards a frumpishly dressed, chaste-looking maiden of white marble on an incongruous plinth of the finest Connemara green. Set back from the path in a recess in the hedge, it was the epitome of unassuming.

'I saw it on the way down.' Her irritation was palpable.

He did not mind overly as he was enjoying his joke.

'Evidently not. Come.'

A cry from along the path stopped them and they turned towards the source, a warm smile upon his face. The girl slowed as she approached, laughing now as if she had caught them hiding. She was glowing from the run, the extra colour complementing her pale skin and emphasising the lingering softness of a face not quite settled in adulthood.

'I'll come too,' she announced in a way that made Lucia reconsider her beauty.

'Not this time, Magda. Go and find Ben. He's with the grapes.'

The brief cloud of sadness dispersed quickly and she was away again, running down the grass, stopping just the once to pick up some leaves which she trailed through the air behind her.

'You've a fan there,' Lucia remarked more archly than she intended.

'Magda? No. She doesn't have that understanding.'

He took her hand as naturally as he would a long-standing friend's – his manner was so at ease that she did not think to resist – and led her past the statue to the obtuse opening in the hedge; an opening which was invisible when the statue was viewed straight on or when approaching from the direction of the Hall. They emerged on to a small rectangle of gravel, taken from the beach, and more hedges. Three paths led away from them, each with a statue as an apparent terminus.

'I like the statues. Did they come as part of a set?'

He ignored her face-restoring sarcasm.

'Actually, yes. And if you can recognise them and work out a story then the path to the centre is as straight as the open road.'

'So long as it's not a road in these parts.'

'Fair enough. Hmm. Let me introduce Faith, Hope, and that little girl is Charity. Take your pick.'

'I have no faith and I abhor charity. The choice is made for me, it seems.'

He had relinquished her hand as she made her choice and they walked freely towards Hope, restoring silence. He could feel her warmth at his left shoulder through his shirt sleeve and he was caught by his own surprise that it seemed good. The yews reared to eight feet on each side, restricting their vision to a tunnel of pale gold, black-green, the washed-out blue of the sky above them, with the white of the statue approaching. The hedges baffled sounds so that the further they walked into the maze the quieter it seemed to become, until even the soft crunch of their own footsteps on the fine gravel sounded as if it belonged to another couple who were following some distance behind. As if to confirm the separation from the world, a blackbird which had been foraging at the base of the hedge flew up in their faces when they were almost upon it, before disappearing in a cascade of curses over the hedge. Startled, she reached for his hand again and did not release it, enjoying the way it wrapped around her own, strongly protective. Leaning into him as they walked, studying his profile when she thought she could, she smelt the work upon him.

'Blackbirds scare themselves. Don't give them heed.'

He stirred at the feel of her soft hand in his roughened paw. So very soft he thought, and he could not imagine she had ever got them dirty or fallen on to tarmac as a child, lifting the skin and planting loose grit beneath. He was easy in his heart as he led her through, moving from Hope to Mercury, turning from Pallas with her owl and Samson with his pillars, deeper into the maze, all the time talking about the life on the estate. She seemed happy to take her time now and they strolled without any haste, lingering at the statues they came to as if under their protection. Finally, they reached Nike who was the herald of the centre. They ducked through the final arch, she gasping as she realised, eyes wide. She could not help but break from him and run out into the clearing, turning first one way then another, smiling and laughing alternately, relaxed now and feeling somehow free in herself, free from the constraints of her life. Here in the heart of the maze none of that seemed to matter.

He spread his arms wide, stepping forward.

'The Cloister.' A smile breaking on his face.

Not a cloister of stone and slate but a living architecture of trained yew, the arcades of rich red trunks, trimmed of all growth, arching and fusing one to another in a tracery of per-

17

pendicular Gothic. The roof above was thick green, cut each year in a feat of ladders and men, the clippings painstakingly brushed down and cleared away. The sky was bounded twenty feet above them by the sharp profile of the apex and the light of the place was somehow both diffuse and pure as if it were delayed on its way to earth, held up by the stillness of the air. Yet even here, in the very core, there was movement as the low sun streamed into the far corner, lifting the last of the frost from the ground in ephemeral vapours.

The honeyed pea-gravel of the paths divided the grass into four, grass left longer now for the autumn and studded with daisies, and converged on a table of black Ashford marble. She was drawn towards it and walked around it, running her fingers along the curved edge, feeling the intense coolness of the stone in the shadow and the warmth of it in the sun. It was so highly polished that the surface of it had begun almost before you realised and it resembled more a liquid, a still pool at night, than an artefact of stone. Into its surface were set constellations, the stars picked out each in its place and the groups delineated in the finest of metal threads which just caught the light enough to lead the eye. She ran her fingertips over it, discerning only a change of temperature as she passed from stone to metal to stone. She was far away in her thoughts of its potential. She stirred as she felt him behind her, her flesh quickening in anticipation.

'Silver?' she asked, turning.

'Platina – it doesn't tarnish.'

Her look was such that he laughed out loud.

'And its value means nothing if you take it away from this place. It's set for the December solstice as seen from here.'

'Amazing. So beautiful. I had not thought to find . . . Well, I expected things to be more –' She dropped her eyes in embarrassment before a smile began to play at the corners of her mouth, '– rustic. Nothing like this.'

'I suppose not.' He considered her and the way she held herself, making his judgement. 'There are many things we

18

hold dear. Perhaps they will seem simple to you, perhaps you'll never rate them as anything. We have time, y'know. In having time there is a chance to see, time to breathe the cool air of the evening, time just to be. Like the sky above. How often did I spend time looking at that before I came here, precious little.'

She too had made her judgements and pressed towards him, her eyes overflowing with intent.

'I think you had better show me what you mean.'

He reached a callused hand, his vine-scented palm brushing her cheek as the tips of his fingers ran into the hair above her ear and down to the nape of her neck. She felt a wave of light-headedness washing over her – she had never thought it would be so easy. The euphoria of her own recklessness drugged her conscience and she went with it. His strange look of remembered sadness did not trouble her then; her body yearned for this feral man and nothing else seemed important.

The distant sound of the stable-yard clock striking twelve broke their languor. Lucia rolled on to her front and with her finger traced the stars again.

'The land here. It isn't profitable, is it?'

He shifted to look more squarely at her. 'Not in the usual sense, no.'

'Do you find it strange . . . that this life is paid for by the world from which you have run away?'

'Who said anything about running away? Perhaps it was a running towards.'

The corners of her mouth drew back, her eyes downcast, 'Oh, well, I guess it feels as if we will be running away, for a time at least.'

Resignedly she stood and began to marshal her clothes into order, tucking in her blouse, frowning slightly, before untucking and making an attempt to smooth out the creases before restoring it once more. He propped himself up on an elbow to watch the process.

'Lunch at one?'

'Yes – but I need to be in the library for drinks at twelve-thirty.'

'Not a bother. We'll have a quick skip through some of the rest of the garden so you've something to talk about if they ask.'

'Is there time?'

'Time enough. The Formal Gardens are quite disappointing now after all, the frost must have been frightful. But you did have a nice walk down to a charming little pool in the woods. The mist was just lifting from its surface and it was quite magical. Come on. You won't set it better than that.'

She looked down at herself one last time.

'No, I suppose not.'

They marched briskly, he leading at a stride whilst she half walked, half ran to keep pace. He fired off salvoes of plant names and aspects of note in the hope that she could take in some detail to embroider any lies she was required to tell. He was sure she would cope, as her intelligence was obvious and she, he suspected, was not unpractised at deception. Even with the stiff pace they were keeping, he could see the poise with which she had arrived in the vinery returning.

They emerged at the edge of a lawn with the picturesque mass of the Hall on the far side. She was chewing slightly at her lower lip as they turned to face one another, her eyes scanning his face. He smiled an odd half smile, his eyes sinking into the stillness of one of his deep silences.

'Well.'

'Well.'

'Goodbye, I suppose.'

He smiled again, more genuinely. She was lovely.

'Go gently now. Your colour is, hmm, a bit healthy.'

Her smile in return nearly broke him. 'Well, whose fault is that?' she teased, her voice low and complacent with pleasure.

'Will you come again?'

'That depends on my husband and Lord Palmer, but I hope so. In the spring.'

'Till then, then.'

'Wait.' As he turned to go she started to rummage in the small bag slung from her shoulder. 'Give me your number and I can text you.'

'Text? If you want to send text, I'd suggest a letter. I haven't a phone.'

He left her horrified at the edge of the lawn and ambled towards the bothy. He laughed to himself at the look on her face and tried out her name a couple of times, rolling it around his mouth like a rich wine. At least one too many syllables, he decided, and thought of other things.

3

In truth she was not the passive subject which her reply to the gardener suggested. Lunch would settle the issue and the final terms would be negotiated: this was more about their acceptance of Inchnamactaire than the other way around. She continued to restore her composure as she crossed the lawn, sniffing at the sprig of rosemary he had slipped through the buttonhole of her shirt. She was aware of a significance she was failing to remember; something for the journey home.

'I smell like a casserole,' she thought, before a smile spread itself across her face as she appreciated his skill. She revelled in the strong, dry musk of the herb. The stakes of the endeavour had been raised, there was no doubt, and the prospect of spending some months in this long-forsaken hole did not seem like the suspension of being they had three hours previously. She had doubted the wisdom of this proposition from the very beginning but the London scene for portraiture was the preserve of an established élite and landscapes had been dead for decades. The pressure of being part of the beautiful set had begun to get to Michael as the months passed and he seemed no nearer to making his name or, as importantly, some money than when he graduated. A spell away from his drinking companions might strengthen his resolve to work, 'trim the fat from his mind,' her aunt and principal trustee had said. 'Though of course you can fund him for ever, but you will resent it no matter the love.'

It was tempting to stay in their comfortable circle of friends, unthreatened by minor talents who wished by association to increase their own value. She hoped this period in the wilderness would test his commitment. Something drastic had to be done, regardless, before the lassitude became set for life. She had wondered at her own place in all this; she was used to the lunches and the galleries and did not know if her own resources would sustain her without her easy society. There was only so much Chopin one could play, after all, although Lady Palmer had been more than happy for her to have free rein with the Bechstein which held court so magnificently in the green music room – 'Better to have it played than sitting idle'– the doubts remained. There would be riding, of course, and swimming, but the emptiness of the land was really quite intimidating. The thought of how it must be in winter made her cold. She was pleased at the prospect of the unexpected pleasures occasioned by the gardens but still, trips home would have to be planned and Michael would just have to get on with it.

Lunch was indeed to be an examination. Not in etiquette, although such could have been the conclusion on being confronted by the full array of silver and crystal, and the attentions of a resentful Alex, the butler, who rarely had to dress at midday and had not quite followed the logic of the request now, something to do with emphasising patronage. Lady Palmer had been insistent, however, and being Lady Palmer did not require logic to support her requests.

Lucia was the last to arrive in the library, a matter of no concern to the Palmers, who did not especially care for time and who, she suspected, knew, as she walked through the door, the cause of her delay. Lady Palmer's smile and welcome profferment of a robust gin gave Lucia the impression that a test had been passed. She took the gin gladly, offering in return her consolations as to the harshness of the frosts.

'Yes, quite frightful,' Lady Palmer replied, gauging Lucia's reaction to the familiar words. 'But when you come in the spring they will be quite transformed. It is my favourite season and so refreshing after the dust of Africa, darling place though it is.'

His remarks earlier about swallows made sense now.

Leaving Michael gasping for air like a slowly drowning man, over in the gothic bay with Lord Palmer, Lucia scanned the shelves. The collection was suitably extensive, rising from the floor to nearly ceiling height, each shelf with its leather dust flange, the colour of martyrdom, guarding the tops of the volumes below it. The recent acquisitions were remarkably similar to any found in her circle at home, coffee-table Taschens, light literature, Whitbread and Impac nominees. She had read them all and the expression of opinions bestowed a natural equality to the exchange, which lessened the feeling of assessment that was only to be expected in the circumstances. She lingered finally over the comprehensive history of art, noticing from the wear on the spines that this was a well-read section. She smiled over to Michael who visibly relaxed, but really she was powerless to help. She could hardly lead Lady Palmer over there. She would save him over lunch, by which time he would know he needed saving and would appreciate it. By which time the sweat of his fear, which was dampening the collar of his new shirt – so nicely toned with the ridiculous tweed he had determined to buy 'to look right,' he had said – would further distract him from any evidence she still bore on her body. Lord Palmer was dressed in stately decline, in a shirt frayed at the collar and at cuffs held together by links of beautifully worked red gold encompassing an emerald of chartreuse. A shirt still bearing the yolk of an errant breakfast egg. A shirt which would be as old as his daughter, whom Michael was to paint next summer when she returned from school. He could have been wearing rags and still he would have been a more impressive figure than her husband, who seemed like a child beside him. The controlled physical power of his bearing was seductive and frightening, much like the gardener's, but the timbre of his voice and the sparkle of his eyes were genuine and warm, whereas those of the gardener's were a different proposition. She shivered at the memory of their closeness, wondering now at herself and what had possessed her.

She could hear Michael expressing some bland opinion on Kandinsky, an opinion she had heard many times after their visit to the archive in Berlin. It was there, verbatim, on their interpretation boards. She wondered now just when he had lost confidence in his own thoughts. The disdain she felt must have registered on her face.

'Do you love your husband?' Lady Palmer was asking.

'I had thought so.'

'We were impressed by the promise of his work.'

'I didn't marry his work . . . Sorry, I didn't mean to be rude.' She was unnerved by Lady Palmer's candour and felt the second reckless urge of the day. 'Only it has always been promise. I don't doubt his creativity either, it's his productivity that worries me.'

'Perhaps with more time . . .'

'He has had so much time.'

'But real time, without distraction.'

'Perhaps,' Lucia conceded, reservedly.

'Don't judge him too harshly just because you have seen giants – he seems a complete dear. Some talents need coaxing, that's all.' She considered Lucia's studied reserve, wondering at its cause. 'Really, his show was one of the finest of his year. He'll surprise you yet, I'm sure.'

She exhaled smoke with vigour, the amethyst boulder on her right hand sending purple light through the ultraviolet of her gin; her smile entirely conspiratorial and utterly indecent, condensing a life of sensuality into one gesture. They chinked glasses and enjoyed a shared silence of understanding. Lady Palmer stubbed out her cigarette and pocketed the yellowed ivory holder, downing her last finger of gin in the same instant. She made towards the corner of the room, pulling open the concealed door in the bookshelves, which swung lightly on its hidden hinges, perfectly balanced and silent.

'Oh no, this place is like a dream world.' Lucia could not help herself.

Lady Palmer's face was suddenly very serious.

'Do not make that mistake, dear, or you will have only nightmares. This is real.'

Then that easy smile broke again like the sun from behind a cloud.

'But we do love our gothick. Boys, Elsie will only burn the meat if we allow the soup to go cold.'

Lunch was a trial, especially for 'dear Michael'. The chilled borscht was a cause of great concern, the spasm of revulsion rippling across his face as the frigid purple touched his cherubic lips for the first time. Lips which had so delicately formed a perfect O only a moment before and puffed genteelly at the spoonful. The hosts, being the acme of politeness when the mood took them, did not appear to notice and changed the conversation from art to current fashions. They had little interest and less knowledge, but they enjoyed the ideas of 'form'. Michael relaxed into his superiority, extolling the virtues of the autumn collections and waxing rapturous over his most recent pair of shoes. As he talked with increasing animation, the wine and the release from the state of tension distorting his sense of propriety, the absurdity of his tweeds became more and more obvious. Initially Lady Palmer thought there might be irony and smiled encouragingly before realising that the earnest response to this was delivered with a conviction which had to be sincere. The twinge of pity she now felt for Lucia flickered in her eyes long enough for Lucia to discern it and it was some relief when the plates were cleared for the next course.

Horses were deemed a safer subject to accompany the smoked pheasant mousse. Lucia had ridden so much from an early age that her legs had even bowed slightly, not that this had ever been a disadvantage. Unfortunately Michael had, as it were, taken the bit between his teeth and was not going to relinquish it without a struggle. Whilst the others debated the merits of introducing the different native pony breeds into the bloodstock, he considered a critique of a recent sub-

Hirstian exhibit with the somewhat predictable title of *The Godfather, Parts 1–3* a valid contribution. The aspic covering of his mousse had taken advantage of his lack of attention and mounted a counter-attack, rebounding and disintegrating into an arc of amber globules which contrasted wonderfully with the pristine linen and quivered slightly every time he emphasised what he thought was a particularly salient point by banging his left hand upon the table, fork firmly ensconced and gripped just below the tines in a pudgy, pink fist not unlike a baby's. Lucia looked fully at him now – when did she last, she wondered, but knew it was some time before he had fattened. He wasn't truly fat, just soft, too much food and indolence. His blond Surrey handsomeness was discernible still, although the chin could have been stronger and that arrogant mouth which had been so enticingly full of confidence when they met appeared now to have become lost amid the jowls and had a Henry VIII mew.

'But the artist had the horses slaughtered specifically; therein lies the genius of the piece – a subversion of the central Catholic paradox that death is beautiful.'

She hated him when he got like this. She hated him with every cell in her body. Then with a compulsive snort she had to disguise as a cough, she laughed at her own unreasonableness; she hated it when he had no opinion and she hated these opinions which were undoubtedly his own. Or perhaps it was just his manner of expression, she thought, excusing herself and her lack of tolerance. The thought of him close to her was almost too much. She knew when they pulled over at the side of the road on the way back to the airport, he would want it, and she doubted at the moment whether she could or whether the newly acquired memories would make it impossible. For better or worse. There had been no better. She looked quickly at their hosts; she blandly benign, he indulgent. They had judged him 'Best in Show' and, indeed, they would not have invited him otherwise. Or been prepared to pay so well. She had grown used to feeling irritated by him, though, and wanted to follow the familiar thought paths. She tried to remember whether she had hated him yesterday or the day before, or whether it had crept in gradually like a slow tide, until the beach of her love was lost under the chaos of the waves and the soft golden sands were hidden, until the waves subsided, leaving behind plastic and dead crabs which would smell and attract flies when the sun heated them. It was difficult, she decided, like a photograph from childhood which has been so much part of life that you no longer know whether or not the memories you have are real or whether you have constructed a memory around the enduring image. She would have to take photographs again.

'Would there be a cellar I could use?' she asked, interrupting Michael mid-sentence.

'Yes, of course, if you need one.' Lord Palmer had warmed to her and was happy to grant her a request which cost him nothing but unsatisfied curiosity.

'I would like to bring my cameras and developing inks and will need a dark room. I prefer to have control myself. I feel if one has gone to the trouble of selecting just the right image and the right instruments to capture a vision then it is foolish to entrust the negatives to someone who was not there and who did not see. It will give me something else to do. They could be included in the arrangement if any pleased you.'

'Why, we had no idea. You have too many bushels, my dear.' Lady Palmer had left the gothic of the gin and become positively baroque with the wine. 'We could have the boys clear the old butchery for you. It has a wonderful stone slab, at least the size of this, and hanging hooks in the vault if you need to put up lines. Plenty of space for you.'

'What's your preferred subject?'

'Oh, like Michael I enjoy portraits and landscape, but I prefer to think of them as objects, in the categorical sense, rather than subjects. I would love to do some studies of the staff here. Perhaps it would be an excellent record without the same time commitment, or the intrusion of a full sitting.'

'By all means, if they are willing. We'll mention it before we go but leave it up to your charm to achieve.'

'They're very free-spirited', Lady Palmer added, 'which is why we love them so.'

The glory of Michael's salvation shone upon his face and his devoted eyes fixed on the wife he loved. His consciousness of social weakness and misplaced wit would blossom over the next days into the predictable bout of self-loathing, to be immersed in drink before a new start could be made. Not for the first time, he was grateful to her. He could be mostly silent now and restrict his contributions to praising the food, which was superb.

* * *

At last they were leaving, pulling out of the drive and through the stretch of dense woodland before the road rounded the head of the giant and returned them to the world they thought they knew. Mostly, she was silent. Michael was talking excitedly; the adrenalin had not yet been exorcised. She was trying to think herself back into London. Remembering her engagements for the coming week and feeling that sense of alienation from the self which can accompany such long journeys. She was enjoying the drive, this unfamiliar car responsive to the pressure from her right foot, the road empty but challenging, the check-in unlikely to be met. It was a good speed to move at. Places seemed more connected when driving. She wanted a feeling of connection now, if only he would cease for a minute.

'How was your tour?' he was asking now.

'Interesting.'

'And?' Impatience evident.

'There was everything but a chapel.'

'Demolished, do you think?'

'Not even a mention of one.'

'Strange . . . Their collection is fine, in an obscure sort of way.'

29

'I'm surprised you noticed.'

'What do you mean by that?'

'Nothing . . . Forget it. The tweed worked well, I thought.'

The lack of noise caused by an artistic sulk filled the car. Not silence. Nor peace. He gnawed at his lower lip and raged to himself. Lucia was glad of the respite. Really, he was much too easy. That look of sadness preyed on her mind, but thinking of him led her on to her own satisfaction and she smiled inwardly at the memory, shifting in her seat as she did so, restless once more.

Dear Anna,

I did not intend callousness; perhaps I have been here too long. Things do reduce to the physical and I missed the nuance of your question. I'm glad to read the cats are well.

So, for the second time of asking: I take no pleasure in it. Paradoxically, I find it harder when it is for food than when for some aesthetic reason. The consciousness of preparing the meat, engaging with the anatomy I suppose, and eating it, knowing what you are eating, and I mean knowing, gives the act a retrospective significance. Nobody here is vegetarian but certainly all the 'land' staff are . . . restrained . . . in their consumption. Whenever I have eaten with the House I have noticed a different attitude, which is understandable as they are one step removed. It is not a question of quantity but how they are whilst they eat. It is part of the life here, but the pleasure of eating is not pure. And it gets harder as each year passes, which again seems wrong. I am easiest when the dogs have killed. The relationship then seems so vital, so necessary, and unreflective. They cannot help it and the act itself seems natural. There is nothing artificial like the accessories of a knife or a trap involved, and the process from first sighting, through the chase, to the death itself seems like a proper progression. What would you say? – That it has a narrative unity, perhaps? That's not to say that it isn't arousing. Not in a sexual way obviously, though I guess unsubtle types might confuse the two. No. But I definitely feel the adrenalin, and the blood flows faster, and there is an indubitable primal recognition there which could be confused with pleasure but which is just death.

My thoughts for the animal? I guess that is the benefit of having lesser souls, that they know nothing about it. Their equanimity can be startling; they seem to bear the expression of a man who is told that he will have to lose a leg and who replies, 'Oh well, I've got another one.' They can be unnervingly calm, and even if it is just the process which induces the appearance of calmness, it is a comforting deception.

I was sorry to read of your trouble with your new boss. Perhaps she will settle down once she feels she has established her authority. Tedious and unnecessary, though, I agree. Do you think a lot of high achievers are quite fragile? I've always assumed it was about proving worth and getting recognition.

These things are trivial by comparison but my life all the same. They have gone until Christmas but have decided to pop back this year for a fortnight from the twentieth. Ours is not to reason why. They haven't done this for years and I think it will be interesting to see how it affects them. I think enduring all the cold and the perpetual wet of winter has an effect on the character; it reminds you of the reality of the country. I don't know what I'm trying to say really, just that it puts the year in context, I suppose. The summer becomes more precious because you know how hard won it has been. I think it makes you more appreciative because the winters here are so unrepentantly selfish. I feel the clouds of oppression gathering like too many covers on the bed. There are good days, genuinely good, when the air is clear and I can lift my eyes to the hills. And fog in the evening, particularly now when it lifts off the grass and drifts through the canopy, or rises from the lough like tentacles, as if the whole water is trying to explore the land for a path of weakness into which it can overflow, drowning the scars of man in the forgetting depths. This is magical. But fog in the morning, impenetrable and permanent, which excludes even the sun so that the whole day is dark, I find the thought of it over the months to come very hard. I know I make the mistake of condensing the dispersed whole into one mass and actually, taken each day, the winter is not as bad as I envisage. Still, for now I am all anticipation.

The artist and his wife came and went. I did not see the man but his name is Michael Berdyaev. I remember a philosopher by the same name, or was it a philologist, I forget. Landscapes and portraits, so a man of talents. If you could ask Patrick about him I'd appreciate it. His wife seemed charming; attractive in a predictable, undemanding way. Difficult to know what she is getting out of all this, though. Perhaps being close to such an artist and involved in that world is enough for some people. Our meeting was too brief to discover much about her character, although I suspect the deep-seated ennui which only a substantial trust fund can induce. You know the signs. She is bright, though, and not yet a lost cause, if she can find something soon that she really cares about.

Adam has been kicking off like a bullock in a stall for the last week now. No cause apparent and I haven't pushed it; I thought it would work out of his system. If it goes on much longer I'll say something, as it's starting to have an effect on the others.

A large skein of geese flew over today, shifting and reforming as they passed. Amazing how they organise themselves – there must have been sixty of them – honking all the while. It reminded me of the swans at Bahir, inaccurate, I know, but that image of approaching the water through those trees, it was this time of year and the ground was golden with fallen leaves, the swans gliding over the oily darkness towards us, oh, but it is branded into my memory. The lake closed in by the ash and the poplars all trembling in the breeze, the low sun leaving the water unlit as it hit the trunks of the trees on the far shore, the avenue of elms arching over the car, the temperature dropping under the canopy of perpetual shade. Gone now of course. The elms and the house. We have some elms on the hill which struggle on. They're stunted by the wind but have probably reached thirty feet all the same. Not like there, though, and I don't think it is just the gigantism of childhood

I am remembering.

I am getting tired, Anna. I must finish.

Love S

4

April was an exorcism; slaying the demons which had arisen in the darkened mists of winter with strong, heartfelt light. It dispersed the ghosts of past lives with a breeze; the warm air of the summer to come and the cold of the winter past experienced together as they buffeted those who walked and worked with it, remaining distinct like the dancers of a tango. Grendel's heirs who daily had prowled abroad, rising up from the waters of the lough and haunting the periphery of vision, reaching cold into the bones of the people of Inchnamactaire with long, amphibious fingers, were shackled now, their wanderings curtailed and infrequent as their strength waned with the failing night. The dread which accompanied their foot-scraping step had been lost and the veil by which they reached land was dissipate and picturesque, brushing the tree-line with the tentative fingers of an offending lover who does not know whether atonement has been made.

April restored the sight of the many. Eyes which had seen enough to navigate the gloamed world but no more, stirred into life as if new blood flowed there. The tightness eased from the temples, and necks and backs unfurled like the croziers of the ferns in the woodland. The brightest leaves of new-born birch burst bud upon the ragged wintered twigs as the sap rose through the phloem in an unstoppable turgor of fertility, forcing life out into the air. Across the estate, trees were tapped for sap and the first wine of the season began its life in jars; palely gold and glutinous, the condensed resilience of *Betula pendula*, entrapped like a genie, only to be released when the year had turned once again. Then, as the canopies thinned, growing sparser with each gust and gasp

of winter air, when their health began to fail, the life withdrawing to the inner being, secreted away in the depths of
root, when the senescent leaves shimmered golden, then the
bottles would be uncorked and the springful vigour of the
tree would be remembered and would comfort those who
feared the shortening of the days.

April raised the dead and the life was good. The foolish
words of winter were forgotten in the sobering light. Rueful
smiles of complicity and forgiveness were 'Good mornings!'
for a week or two as the people of Inchnamactaire stepped
back into their selves, filling their skins again like a bear wak-
ening from hibernation and finding a store of apples preserved under the snow. Blinking at the brightness of this
foreign sun, returned from its travels, not quite remembering
the rituals of orthodox observance.

He spent the days of his own in the woodland pasture,
walking among the massed trunks of the silver birch at its
edges, and the coppicing of hazel within. He loved the light
here; the woodland grass seemed to generate its own and
glowed from the ground. Lesser celandine ran through it like
a million citrines, the light reflecting points on a wave of
green at sunset on the western shore. He craved it like a starv-
ing man craves food. Everything was pleasing. The cool
dampness to the air made breathing relaxed and easy; the
verdant light soothed the eyes and made them peaceful until
closing them became an intrusion – a regrettable caesura
which fractured the bond of mind and place. The air was
stilled but not foetid; it moved with a gentleness redolent
with memories. Happy memories of the smiles of strangers
on railway platforms in the days before mobile phones. Of
felicitous glances which in their freedom to mean nothing
conveyed more truth than a thousand 'I love yous'. Of the
first sip of whiskey, triple distilled and generously poured by
the hand of a friend, with fifteen years of history in the glass
and a litany of forgiveness for the past. Of the last bars of *Four
Last Songs*, so many years ago in that strange labyrinth of the

35

Barbican. The bizarre, curved wood-laminate of the walls encapsulating the hundreds like insects in amber. He was there with a friend, he remembered; they were beginning life as best they could, *andante*. The orchestra were tuning and the anticipation was religious as they strove for the convergence of sound which would make the many one. As the musicians tuned, each with an ear attentive to their master, the audience too coalesced into one needy being that breathed with the same expectation of fulfilment, until the two, orchestra and audience, went out into the night, lighting cigarettes.

It seemed so long ago to him now that he struggled to reconcile the self who had been so social with the self who now stood, his back curved against the trunk behind him. He struggled to think consecutively at all, the detail of daily living jostled at the edges of his mind and frequently burst through. He reached out an automatic hand and smoothed the head of Sally who had returned to him and who sat, with eyes imploring and tail twitching, hoping for more. He settled on his haunches, a position he could maintain for hours, his weeding position, and keeled his back against the tree. He loved the silence of dogs. He knew the contours of the head without thought and glanced briefly as her eyes closed with pleasure. Like smoking, the familiar action helped him to think, as if enough of his brain were distracted and could no longer sabotage the rest.

The moon pond was beautiful, and he did not himself have the ego to remember each time he looked at it that this was his creation. Instead it had been born into the world and, like a child, had taken on its own being and developed without regard to its creator. The pool itself was one hundred feet in diameter, the sides cut sheer into the depths so that they did not distract the eye. Bright woodland grass grew around the edge, softening the geometry of the curve and reflecting on the water, further disguising the construction. Set back from the water's edge, twenty-four silver birch were planted in a double circle like the hours of a clock or the months of a year.

That idea was not his own. Once, shortly before the Strauss, he had stayed in an Adam square in London. The central garden 'for the use of residents, access by key' had been buggered about. The same esteemed residents had demonstrated their refinement by felling one of the magnificent planes and replacing it with an especially mediocre sculpture by an especially famous if one-dimensional sculptor. Incongruous shrubberies of the municipal lavatory school were dotted here and there as if the residents' committee had watched where Foodles the lapsang-souchong had lifted his leg as he wandered around; Foodles was a master of feng shui after all. But despite the violations and the indignities the rationale of the original design screamed out to any who had the time to listen. He had time that week certainly, as he stood in the window of the private hospital, watching the people eating lunch or reading in the garden, so he fantasised about restoration and wondered whether, if it were whole again, anybody would lift their eyes from the ground before them and stop, just for a moment or two perhaps, and consider the eloquence which they ignored. Towards the end he was allowed a key too, and eagerly went down, unlocking the iron gate with the large heavy key, feeling the resistance in the un-oiled mechanism and the blur of rust as the bolt bridged the gap to the casing. The moist air was heaven after the sterile conditioning of the room. He stooped and slipped off his shoes and walked the perimeter, pacing it out for later drawings, the cool grass pressing up between his toes and staining his soles green. He walked from tree to tree and from tree to root-mound – all that remained of a lost hour – and from the ordinal points to the centre, counting each to check accuracy, enduring the enforced slowness of laboured breath, his spirit willing vigour. At the felled centre he turned and faced east first, then west, north then south, scanning the façades of the square for detail and symmetry, grieving for the lives which no longer lingered behind the reflecting panes of the casements, which today concealed solicitors and architects. The statue he decided

37

was at seven, although from his window he had considered it to be at one. It was no less hideous on closer inspection – a soul-draining presence.

The birch trunks reflected as pillars of silver in the darkened waters. In spring and autumn they were magnificent, as a corolla of pale green or buttered gold coalesced in the centre of the pool. Summer was not their best season. Even the lightness of the birch in full leaf was too great for the water to support and the beauty was lost in complication. A winter's night was its zenith. The naked trunks were lit by the moon of a full cycle; the first after equinox was perfection itself. As it wrenched itself clear of the hill where it hung low and huge for so long before arcing high and filling the pool with liquid silver.

Now as he sat, he could see the grass was studded with the darker spikes of the bluebell leaves, the buds just beginning to colour. Another month and the evening sky would have come to earth. Beyond the birch hours lay a circle of yew, pierced at the quarters. He had grown it all from the darkest form he could find among the hedges of the maze, yet each had found its own way. They had been left uncut after the sixth year and the irregular growth naturalised the circle.

The pool lay within the wood and for now the shapes of the oak standards could be seen from within the circle. He hoped that in time, once the birch matured, this would be its own world, not referenced to anything. The paths of arrival forgotten until the yew was breached for leaving.

He was released as he sat there, as his eyes drifted over the waters, the cloud reflected, and he wondered, as he always wondered – and knowing the physics had never damaged the feeling – how the illusion of depth could be created by a mirror.

The people of Innisbeag were kindly and simple. Among them grew up Medh who, it was said, was the most beautiful girl ever to live on the island, or in the land of the yew, or indeed the whole world. Somhairle loved Medh with a deep love and when he caught sight of her he would stop whatever he was at and shout, 'Medh, I love you with a love as deep as the ocean, a love of which the bards can only sing and never know!' But she would not. Medh had a haughty spirit; the reflections in the still pools of the island had sickened her and she loved her untouched skin, her hair like a raven's wing, reflecting light from unseen depths. Somhairle was a prince among men, broad and long of limb, graceful in body and tongue, with hair flowing, the colour of a hero's. She grew annoyed at his attentions. After a year or so, when Somhairle called out, 'Medh, I love you with a love as deep as the ocean, a love –,' she turned on him with fire in her eyes. 'You say you love me so, but all I hear is the wind disturbing the sleep of the willows! Go, find your depths of the ocean and bring me a trophy from the kingdom under the sea, the kingdom of promise. Then, when you return, the bards will chant of your great love and I, moved by their words, will be yours.'

At once, Somhairle's heart was torn with the hope of his love and the despair at the challenge. No one had returned from the kingdom of promise and, in truth, he did not know how to find it. He was a practical soul however, and thought he could consider the issue better from the shore. He approached each of the fishermen in turn, retelling his plight and begging from them the use of a boat, just for the turning of two tides. Not with laughter but with sorrowful faces did they answer his pleas, each in their turn refusing, though it broke their hearts to do so. Somhairle was well loved and Medh the only girl whose beauty could match him. As night fell he was left alone on the beach and sat on a well-smoothed rock, the land behind him, and wept. The waves came and soothed his feet, the incandescent edge frothing over his toes and circling his ankles before easing its grip and retreating, laden with his tears. A stream came down from the woods and ran through the rocks to the sea. The beasts of the forest would follow the stream at night and in the peace of the moon, graze the seaweed or forage for crabs, whatever was their way. This night was no different and as they picked their way along its bed, they heard the cries of Somhairle and were deeply moved

39

with compassion. A young doe approached and asked his trouble. When the story was told, and it was not long in the telling, the beasts withdrew some distance for counsel. When the matter was decided the doe returned to Somhairle.

'You are loved among all the people of Innisbeag, the most. Medh is lost but our wisdom says your love may save her. We will lend you our skins for a year from dawn tomorrow. Take osier and build a currach and seek the kingdom with our blessing. If you are not returned in twelve moons our curse will be upon Innisbeag and none shall be spared.'

Somhairle's tears were of joy and he rose swiftly and cut osier from the stream bank. When he returned, a neat bundle of skins were folded on the rock for him. These he fastened through with thorn around the frame of willow and, as the sun rose in the east, he pushed his coracle out on to the golden path before him, praising the moon whose whispers drew the tide before him. He sailed out with hope as the sun climbed high above him and all sight of land was lost, he knew he would be back within a month and Medh's bed would be his. As night fell his hope was dimmed but he was pleased that he still lay in the path of the sun as it sank below the sea. Tomorrow, perhaps, he would reach the gates. He was staring into the darkening waters and as he did so he became aware of two eyes staring back. A seal with a friendly sort of a face popped up its head through the waves.

'You must be Somhairle,' the seal said, before Somhairle could introduce himself. 'Your tears cried your story in the waters from Innisbeag.'

'Can you show me the kingdom of promise, my friend?'

'I can that, but you'll never find it in your craft. Come into the water and I will lead you there. Take a hold.'

So, as the moon climbed high into the night sky, Somhairle climbed into the waters and slipped below the silvered surface, the curse of the skins forgotten. He grasped the flipper of his guide and it dived and dived until Somhairle cried out with the pain of it.

'Take me back,' he begged the seal. 'You're killing me.'

The seal laughed and flashed a sharp-toothed smile,

'How else will you enter the kingdom, foolish one?' and on he dived, harder now, grasping Somhairle's wrist with an indisputable hold.

After what seemed a lifetime, Somhairle and the seal came to an arch of rock under the waves through which a golden light flowed out and the distant strains of beautiful voices singing could just be heard. The seal released him, and without a backward glance, swam into the night. Somhairle stepped through the gates and entered the kingdom of forgetting. His eyes were dulled by the beauty of all he saw, his mind numbed with the incessant meeting of all his pleasures. No sooner had a desire formed in his mind, than it was gone, and he was lost in the endless moment of enjoyment.

On the shore of Innisbeag, the animals waited, facing the waves. The sun was setting behind them and lighting the path to the kingdom. The moon rose and a murmur began among them which grew and swelled until the chant of it could be heard from far off. With the rhythm established they formed a line and with heads down began to walk the shore of the island. The people rose from their beds at the sound of the wind, which howled from a world unsettled, and beat their houses from all directions at once. Doors were fastened doubly and still no one slept.

The fearful people greeted the morning with the whiskey eyes of sleep-free nights. They went out into the light, each from their house, rubbing their eyes at the brightness; it took them a moment or two to realise. The sores which covered their bodies grew red and blotched and itched like fury. But the people got no satisfaction when they scratched; the sores wept or bled then itched some more. No part of their bodies was spared, the sores even reaching up to and into their hair, making it greasy and dull. There were no children born that year.

As the months passed, news of the troubles spread as traders called at the island once only, and would not return. The proud people who had been dressed so finely in soft wools and embroidered linens had to put on rough cloth of hemp or calf-skin, cloth which raised the skin of their sorrows, so that the worst afflicted went naked rather than suffer more. Medh suffered more than any other and could not bear the touch of any cloth against her skin; it was said she even slept standing. Her private beauty was laid bare but it raised no desire in any man and to women, she was only pitied. Her full hair, so very black as a raven's wing, fell in clumps, and what remained was matted and dull.

One day, if days have meaning in the other kingdom, Somhairle found himself near the arch of rock, which he recognised. This itself was a surprise to him as he realised he had never seen the same place twice in this world. He sat himself on a rock facing this arch, peering into the dark which lay beyond it, trying with his whole self to remember why he might have seen it before. He thought so hard that he was without the distraction of desire for the first time and his head ached with the effort. He may have been sat there a week when he felt on the current coming through the arch two songs of great sorrow, sung in voices he recognised. One song was sung by the beasts and one by the people of Innisbeag, but each lamented the same thing.

His eyes lifted from the surface of the pool and into the evening woodland around him. Sally, who had been sleeping, curled with her nose tucked into her tail, opened her eyes at his movement, to see if more was expected. He rolled himself a cigarette, and she stretched herself out, first through one back paw and then the other, her tongue curling out in a yawn until the tip brushed the roof of her mouth, before shaking and wagging whilst she waited. He uncurled himself from the tree and stretched himself out, blinking the thoughts from his eyes and sucking greedily at the roll-up.

The artist and his wife were due that evening and he had to be there at the Dower to meet them. The range of his lodge was the same model as that of the Dower's and effective if tended by a person who knew how to coax the best out of it but shy with strangers. It had been considered less trouble in the long run if the new arrivals received instruction immediately. He had lit the other fires the day before and cracked the windows to allow the air through. It hadn't been lived in since Sam's time – just over two years now – but it was a solid sort of place and would be fine for this evening. Sam was dearly missed still when people were together and his low, enduring laughter would not be there, in the background after all others had ceased to laugh. It had taken three coats of paint to cover the last trace of him. His furniture had been burnt and the floors were stripped down, and it was smart and clean now. Furniture had been brought up from the Hall that morning whilst he was there relighting the fires for the coming day. It would be comfortable while preserving the 'space' which the artist had insisted was important in word, and letter, and fax, and there was 'nothing in green', just as requested.

He could tell by the fading light that he was going to be pushing it if they were not to arrive before him, and he picked up his pace and turned his collar against the cold wind which was stirring from the east. Sally was glad to be moving again and trotted along, sometimes before and sometimes after. He realised he hadn't seen Phlebus for some time, so he whistled as he went; not that it mattered, Phlebus would find a way but he fancied the company all the same. As he crested the last hill before the Dower he could see a silver car crunching up the pea gravel and swinging round the corner of the house. He paused long enough to roll and drew twice before ambling down, fortified. It struck him as strange that nobody had got out of the car. Then, as he got near enough for them to notice his approach through the gloom, Lucia leapt from the passenger's side and ran towards him.

'Thank God you're here! You've got to do something!'

Her evident distress gave him pause and even the dog held back from the greeting which was customary. She grabbed him by the wrist and pulled him towards the rear of the saloon.

'We've had an accident.' The tone was right, and meant

perhaps for Michael, who had got out and who was now following behind, but a flicker of the eyes said more. She lifted
the lid of the boot which sucked against the unworn seal, and
there, huddled in a small space cleared of boxes and bags and
the miscellany of travel, lay a medium-grown jill. She blinked
her eyes against the yellowed light which shone out as the
boot swung open, and as if wakened from sleep, she started
to scrabble frantically, pulling with her front legs. She was
beautiful with oval, almond eyes of ancient understandings; a
spirit of the fields and woodland edges, furtive and alert.
Now, her beauty was tortured as her soul sought for the
speed which would take her from danger, betrayed by back
legs which fell away, lifeless. He ran his eyes over her until
just above the pelvis he could see the tell-tale kink of an
impossible spine, cast in high relief by the nearest light.

'For fuck's sake, it's just a bloody rabbit!' Michael raging
and pacing, to the boot and away in short steps upon the
gravel, drawing needfully at a Marlboro Light.

'She's not a rabbit.' And he moved his hand towards her as
she pulled desperately with her front paws, her nails catching
in the carpet of the boot floor. Yet, as he slipped his hand
under the ears which were flattened tight against the neck,
and his fingers slid round her until he could hold, she stilled
and her breathing calmed. He eased his left hand up, under
her breast so that he could lift her, supporting her weight.

'Can you help . . . her?'

'Yes. Stay here.' He walked away, around the corner of the
house; the hare still in his arms. 'Sally, stay there.'

Michael was grinding his butt-end into the gravel with his
right toe, his hands thrust into his pockets, when the gardener
came back, cradling the hare as before. He looked from him to
her and back, before laying the hare down reverentially on
her side before the dog.

'Leave.' His hand arching over Sally's head, her tail beating
twice against the ground.

'That was badly done.'

44

'Oh, for Christ's . . .' Michael began, before the look he received silenced him.

'I don't take life lightly.' The words taut and strained, then a breath. 'I was asked to come so that I could show you how to tend the range. I suggest we do that and then I can leave you to settle in. Would you like a hand in with the bags first?'

They left all the bags in the hallway to be sorted at leisure. Little was said. When that was done, he set to with the range, stacking the chamber with paper twists and kindling. Lucia perched herself on the table edge, legs slightly splayed, turned towards him and attentive. Michael paced from room to room, but was shouting reports through or down, wherever he had reached. Just as this was getting annoying, Michael returned to the kitchen.

'You won't believe the bathroom. Not even a bloody shower! It's so unhygienic to sit in a bath!'

'Are you ready to pay attention now? Good. This will provide for the radiators and the hot water for washing. You can cook on the top too. There's a letter on the table, aye just by your leg, explaining other arrangements. You can pick up a meal at lunch in the undercroft. Nothing fancy but it is sustaining. Now, when you light it, you need the flues like this . . . Watch! . . . but the trick is to keep it lit. You'll find a clamp round the side of the house, next to the coal shed. Feed it last thing at night and turn the vents like this.'

Michael's mind was still on the bathroom, Lucia had drifted elsewhere too but to where he did not know.

'You don't have to listen. But if you don't, you will be cold and you will be hungry. Now, feed it first thing in the morning and reverse the flues until it catches. Then turn them down.'

It was pitch black as he left and his annoyance was as deep. Sally, sat by the hare still, wagged as he approached. The hare was cold now and starting to stiffen. His heart felt leaden within him as he grieved the wasted death, reaching in his pocket for a hook with which to carry her back. He passed it through behind the Achilles tendon of each heel, pressing it against the loose skin until it paled at the point and parted over the metal tip. He settled the T-bar into his fingers, the metal cold against his flesh, and turned out, over the park to home. He would bury it that night under the moon, this spirit he had never before killed, covering its rest with a cairn of stones to keep it safe from the foxes and dogs.

She watched his silhouette to the gate, the shadow at his heel merging into his leg. She chewed at her lower lip, half registering the sound of a bottle being uncorked. She was glad he had not asked what happened on the road, the running hare, not turning to the left or the right, Michael losing patience, already angry from the argument they were having, not stopping until she was screaming at him. The light was blocked as her husband entered the room and he came behind her, placing a hand at the small of her back and kissing the nape of her neck, making her wince.

'What now?' he asked, hurt and immediately annoyed.

'Just a shiver.' She took the glass of red wine, dark as old blood, and sipped at it lightly. 'One from the cellar?'

'Yes'.

'It's good. Very good.' She turned her head towards him, the shadow of a smile at the corners of her mouth. 'I think the time here will be well spent, don't you?'

'I hope so.' Glasses clinked and they sipped again. 'That wasn't the best beginning exactly.' He looked sheepish now, the closest she would get to an apology tonight. 'I hope they're not all as dour as him.'

'I'll talk him round. He'll be fine.'

* * *

5

It had been three days since anyone except the House staff had seen the couple for more than an instant. They secluded themselves in the Dower and sought no company. So exclusive was their habit that a murmur had begun, 'What and when is he going to paint?' and, 'There's nothing but the four walls, unless he's painting her, do you think?' Not that the House was any more satisfied. Elsie in particular was beside herself at their comings and goings with barely a word of gratitude.

Michael and Lucia were busy, though. They both enjoyed order and were sensitive to disturbance. They had started to unpack their things until, as they found places for the artefacts they had brought, talismans which gave them a sense of continuity, they realised that the furniture was not rightly placed. A day was spent adjusting things, shuffling arrangements of chairs like pieces on a chessboard, for sterile games in which nothing would be taken. The dining room became a lounge as the light was better in the evening, and half the lounge disappeared upstairs so that a second lounge could be created there with views across the park. Lucia had spent another half-day in there, lost out of the window in the comings and goings of the clouds upon the mountain. At last she finished reordering the books on the shelves and, pretext exhausted, returned to the fray. Michael had gutted the study in her absence to provide a studio and was busy setting out his wares. Pique at her own dilatoriness seeped into her tone, which as ever garnered no response, Michael being tone deaf. She wondered at her hesitation in claiming this lovely little room with its sweet corner fireplace with the rose motif in the ironwork. It would have made a perfect quiet room, here at the extremity of the house, where she could have just *been*. Now Michael would infest it with his business and concentration and the beautiful stillness would be forced out. Where does the silence go? she wondered. Were the walls like a reservoir, a battery charged with peace? At night when the lights were turned off and the door was shut, the peace would flow out into the air and restore as much as was possible, as much as all these alien presences would allow. She had enjoyed Michael's studio at night for as long as she had known him. In the semi-darkness, the strange essences of the paints would mingle, and she would imagine colours and moods to go with the smell. By day these moods were lost, too subtle to resist the dominance of the eyes. She would try to place the remembered mood next to the picture she thought had provoked it, but even the geography of the room seemed altered.

It must take years for a room to accumulate such a store of tranquillity, years of continuous peace. Sam had never used the room, as far as anybody was aware. When the house came to be cleared it was as bare as it had been when the house was first built. The hearth was clean and there was no dust. Only the faded pattern of the wallpaper on the window embrasures recorded the passing of time. It may have been the care of the builders which had imbued it with such an air – the satisfaction of the men had passed from their bodies through their hands and been pressed into the mortar at the tips of the trowels. She had not thought of the builders and she knew nothing of Sam, but she loved this room and would have to enjoy it now when Michael was elsewhere.

'I wonder how long it takes before it is lost?'

'What?' Michael was annoyance and knitted brows over an easel.

'Sorry. I didn't realise I was thinking out loud. Nothing.'

'I'm nearly ready for a gin.'

'Yes, it must be that time.' She turned and kissed him over the obstacle and went out to pour drinks, her eyes far away.

He watched her drift out, the scowl spreading like ripples on the flat surface of his face. He chewed at a nail, spitting the bits into the fireplace; she could be very irritating, he decided. How was he ever to paint with her hanging around looking maudlin. He could kill for the gin.

* * *

He was late home that evening and the sky was violet with light, sooty clouds streaming across in lines like homeward bound cars. The colours were fading from the rest of the world, though as he looked at the grass it still seemed green. A dew of the early season was settling upon it and a darkening stain was spreading out from the toes of his boots as he walked almost noiselessly with long, easy strides. It had to be one of his favourite times, with the thinnest of crescent moons revealing itself, as yet outshone by Hesperus, low and brilliant; he was peaceful. The dogs were subdued from hunger and kept close; he would feed them first, as was only fair after their wait. He put his hand to the gate wondering what he himself would eat, and on to the gravel, which yielded pleasingly under his feet with a progressive crunch. He turned to close it after the dogs but they were stuck fast to the post, their noses twitching furiously with whatever advantage they had.

'Come now,' he said quietly.

Phlebus cocked his leg before passing. He approached the door with caution and pressed upon it lightly, then it swung. Years since it had warped until the snicket would not close from inside unless a vigorous hip or shoulder were applied. He kept the dogs to heel with a hand signal and entered the hallway. The lamps were unlit. He turned left into the parlour, carrying the door with his shoulder and reaching for the matches which he knew to be on the window-sill. They had been moved but not far, as if whoever had replaced them had tried to find the same spot. He struck a light and raised the lamp.

49

There was electricity on the estate, there had been from the beginning; a hydro-system of diverted streams which ran from the mountain perpetually, and from the turbine to the lough. All the other cottages had power enough but here, at the extremity, they had never bothered. He didn't really care. It had been odd at first but only as one thing among many of his new life.

The glow wavered as if the darkness had grown too great to be opposed, then resolved, throwing out enough to reveal the room. It was mainly square, broken by the large chimney-breast and a hearth which always burned brightly. Another door led through to a kitchen, and under it the faint glow of moonlight could be seen. It was stone flagged and punishing to bare feet but in front of the fire was laid an Armenian carpet, the patterned wool deep in colours and pile. A long Knole settee faced the hearth, its brocade frayed at the corners of the cushions. One foot had gone astray during its life but an early edition of *Great Expectations* was substituting admirably. Two high-backed chairs closed the circle. One was low-slung and his perfect fireside chair. He could stretch out his legs and rest his feet by the flames. The deep cushions were firm but yielding, and carried the tired weight of his limbs without complaint. The facing chair was larger, with a feather seat he had never liked. She sat hunched in this, her knees drawn up against the clear evening cold, her arms wrapped around her shins protectively. Her face held things he did not wish to know.

He placed the lamp upon the mantel and made the fire, stacking the split curves of well-seasoned beech, like the bleached ribs of some immense beast, across the resinous strands of pine and the papered curls of birch bark, silvered within and copper without. He had intended to do it that morning, knowing he would be late in but somehow it had been missed. He could feel her eyes upon him as he worked and he wondered at the restraint of the hounds who stood, square-legged, watching without movement. The fire guttered and flamed and its light was added to the room. He carried the lamp through to the kitchen and added water to the bowls of food for the dogs, who came in a hurry, nails clicking on the flags, at the familiar sound.

He reached down two glasses and half filled them with whiskey. Tucking the bottle under his arm he grasped the glasses in one hand and with the lamp in the other, pulled the door to behind him. She had not moved. His eyes had adjusted to the light and he thought she had the dirty face of someone who had been crying. She took the proffered glass with an automatic hand, forgetting she did not drink whiskey, her fingers brushing his as she received it. They chinked bottoms and he sank into the chair and faced her. The flames bathed them in an orange glow and cast fantastical shadows on the walls behind them. A mouthful of whiskey warmed him and his body received the sugars with gratitude. Tongues of flame licked under and around the beech which flished gently in response and glowed along the caressed edge. He cradled the glass in his hand, the amber liquid glowing through his parted fingers as if he held the fire itself, his eyes unfocused beyond his feet, hearing the fire, smelling the sweet burning of the birch as it mingled with the fumes of the drink, with its memory of southern sun enclosed in a casket of oak, shut away in darkness. He knew she could not see his face too well, the lamp was behind him, and he could check her progress in this silence before lapsing back to thought.

Lucia had not expected this, though now, as she thought, she had had no expectations beyond seeing him again. She had not expected this room, so sparse, monastic with bare walls and floor, so luxuriant. She had kicked off her shoes and pressed her feet into the rug, revelling in the wool which explored her toes and tickled her soles. She had stepped from the cold stone to the rug and back, her mind quickened by the contrast, and plunged her eyes into the colours of the pattern; the blue like a darkening night, the red of setting blood. The chair she sat in was proportioned like a throne and enclosed

51

her despite her height. The dark bronze of the brocade captured her eyes in depths which seemed to absorb all light.

She sipped her drink, which was smoother than she remembered, and studied him for a sign. The fluid light lapped his face and receded like waves on a shore, making it unfixed. She thought he might be smiling but his eyes were closed to her and she could not be sure. She wavered now, uncertain. Doubt and foolishness had entered the room hand in hand and were creeping towards her. She drained her glass in defiance and they smiled acknowledgement and retreated. The clock in the hallway whirred and chimed; eight bells. She slipped out of her chair and out of her clothes, her eyes upon him all the while.

* * *

They lay on the carpet together, her head cradled at his shoulder. She could smell the day's labour upon him, warm and earthy and comforting, as she looked out over the firm expanse of his chest which rose and fell steadily, listening to his still racing heart within. His eyes were somewhere near the ceiling; besieged by thoughts, chaotic and persistent.

She spoke properly for the first time. 'Are you always so silent?'

He sighed and turned his head to her before easing his arm out from under her so that he could prop himself up. He reached for the whiskey and poured two more glasses, sipping at his to moisten his tongue.

'Sometimes I have nothing to say,' but he softened the words with a smile. He looked down over her, her beautiful long limbs with their slow curves, and could not resist reaching his hand, the forefingers bent like an El Greco saint bestowing a blessing, and tracing the line of a rib. She gasped quietly at the coldness of the touch, the skin rising in goose bumps.

'Why were you crying?' His tongue remembered the salt of dried tears when he had kissed her eyes.

'I don't know really. Tiredness?'

He let it pass, sipping once more. He smoothed hair from her face and bent forward, kissing her gently on the mouth.

'You're very beautiful. Even in sadness.'

This time their sex was leisured and tender. He held her gaze throughout until she stiffened under him, her head thrown back, crushing his supporting hand into the floor. He arched his back and kissed down her taut neck until he submitted also.

They lay entwined, stilled and silenced. But the silence was good; a silence of peace between them which they broke only occasionally with quiet words. They traced each other's curves with slow fingers, learning a new anatomy of love; a body memory of another. Her frustration with what she thought of as her mistake held no power over her as she lay there, and she knew it would destroy the moment to try to explain. It had no place. She fought the urge to bring him closer, wanting to feel as free with her words as she felt with him physically. She knew already that she was starting to expect more. Her marriage had not been how she had expected, the uncomfortable knowledge of herself she had acquired and Michael, well, it was beyond the personal. She knew he had not deceived her, she had managed that on her own, the child she had been. This man with his hand upon her thigh, sending shivers through her, would not want to know and she guarded herself against the beginnings of hurt.

'I should take you back,' he said, finally.

'I know.'

'Were you out for a walk?'

'Yes . . . But it's so easy to get lost in the dark.'

They laughed gently together.

'Come on. I've got something in the shed for just such emergencies.'

They dressed quickly, and he guarded the fire and trimmed down the lamp whilst she finished. They went out through the kitchen and whilst he scribbled a note on a piece of paper, she got acquainted.

'What are they called?'

'Sally, Phlebus.' He pointed in turn.

'Flea bus? No.'

'Phlebus. I inherited him. I know, but he was too old to change it.'

'I've never seen a dog so dark.'

'He is extraordinary.'

'Sally's very pretty. Has she some setter?'

'Perhaps, yes.' He shrugged and whistled them out with him to the yard.

'Now do you want to ride in the car or pillion?'

She hooted in delight as he started the bike and she climbed up behind him, wrapping her arms around his waist.

'Hold on tight – it'll be a bumpy ride.'

'My favourite!' she shouted above the noise of the engine, as he slipped it into first and pulled out of the shed, laughing at her unexpected lewdness.

They cut across the park until they came to the bottom of the hill behind which the Dower lay. The wind was up and the billowed trees would help to muffle the noise of the engine, so loud to them, and so alien to the estate at this time of night.

'I'll drop you here – you're just over that hill.'

They kissed once more before parting. He gave her the benefit of the headlamp until she reached the brow, then wheeled the bike round and headed for the bothy with his note. 'Nothing like declaring your business,' he thought as he trundled past the other cottages.

His clock was striking eleven when he returned to his lodge and after backing the bike into the shed, he sat on the step and spent a few minutes with the hounds and a cigarette. There had been things he had wanted to do tonight; a letter to Anna, some reading. This affair, if such it was to become, would have to be worked out properly. He smelt of the day's labour, having missed his bath but that would have to wait until morning. It was all he could do to drag himself to bed.

54

6

He woke to the sound of footsteps on the stairs, footsteps he recognised. The restrained light which shone above the shutters was enough to hurt his eyes and his head set up a dull throbbing beat with which the boots on the wooden treads kept time, adding to the agony. He needed his coffee and he needed a cigarette. Most of all, he should have eaten something the previous night; it had just not seemed important at the time. Nausea hunted him, as it did when he was woken suddenly from a deep sleep, and he reached for the water with which he had had the foresight to provide himself. He struggled up on to one elbow, turning towards the door, and sipped at the glass. The water was cold enough to crack teeth and brought him round instantly. A head appeared at the door.

'Ben, how are you?'

'Morning, squire. Not bad in myself.'

'Don't call me that, it brings back bad memories. Stop craning and come in.'

He squared himself and struggled up to sitting, noting it was colder than usual. 'I didn't expect to see you. Did you not get the note?'

'No, the note was fine too.' Ben was distracted and hesitant.

'Well, I don't suppose you came to pass the time of day when there's work to be done; it looks a grand day for it.'

'Ah, yes. It's the artist. We can't get the work done. Could you come?'

A grand day for problems, he thought, and swung his legs out of bed, putting on his jeans and retrieving his shirt from the day before, something he would never do, which lay crumpled on the floor next to the chair. He caught the smell of her on it, sweeter than his own and giving him a hidden smile of memory as he pulled it over his head. Ben was looking with surprise at him as his head appeared at the neck of the shirt. On a normal day he would not have bothered to explain but there was nothing normal about today.

'I'll sort you out then come back. I don't think I'd better work today.' He opened the shutters as he passed them, allowing a shaft of strong yellow light to blaze across the floor. Its heat was immediate and welcome, and when he had found a pair of socks in the wooden chest of drawers which stood in the alcove next to the hearth, he returned and sat on the floor, bathing his back in it whilst he pulled them on. He smiled at Ben who was looking less sheepish now.

'I'll need coffee, though, before I do anything.'

At the bottom of the stairs the dogs greeted him for the second time; that at least he had managed before crawling back to bed.

'Did you walk?' he threw back over his shoulder.

'No, I cycled round.'

'Good, I'll join you.'

He reached for the coffee pot and his body went through the motions without the need for thought. Other thoughts were penetrating slowly, Ben was chatting in the background, giving him the detail and the fully realised opinions of all the aggrieved. He lifted the cover of the boiling plate and set the pot on to it. There would be no porridge in the slow oven but there was an end of a loaf in the bread bin, and he sliced this in two, smearing each half with butter before ladling on a good spoonful of thick loganberry jam. He slid the plate on to the table and turned back to the range. Finally, the thought clarified.

'Fuck. The fire's gone out.' He opened the chamber and poked around but there was only a little life, an orange fleck here and there on the few embers remaining in the soot-blackened void. He swung it to and checked the hot plate but the residual heat would not be enough. A second fuck. He padded through to the parlour and returned with the whiskey. Ben's look of confusion was transformed and a smile of conspiratorial understanding spread across his face.

'Drink?'

'Just a finger.'

* * *

The cycle over was enjoyably sociable; the landscape changed so quickly at this time of year that every day brought something new to see. The woods on the hill were greening, though here and there a bare patch announced the presence of oak or ash, always so late to wake up after their deep sleep of recovery from their exertions of the previous season. A light breeze cooled the air and lifted ripples on the lough and each was tipped with light like unnumbered constellations spread out over the dark waters' sky. At the top of a slight rise, they squeaked their bicycles to a halt and looked out over the water to the hill beyond. The lightest of clouds were forming round the giant's head like sad memories and their shadows played down the neck and over the shoulder. They rolled and smoked, breathing deeply between draws as if to capture as much of the scene as possible. It seemed to him he was looking at it for the first time in years. The bright green of young, soft bracken shone out above the trees amid the darker heather, a patchwork of light and shade born from the earth. Movement caught his eyes and there, from the tree line, rose the blackened shapes of two large birds, riding a thermal of the morning sun. One was more adept than the other and rose quickly, leaving its companion far below. If it flapped its wings he did not see, they were too far for such detail, and as it passed before the heather or a cloud shadow he struggled to follow it.

He knew they were ravens, although the wind was carrying their calling away, on to the hillside, to be lost among the rocks. Ravens had been his first love many years past, so unexpected and other. There had been a country fair in the village. Mad hippie pipers were throttling tunes from instruments of ancient sensibility, whilst their bearded friends called Peter and Trevor, white, middle class, fathers accountants and mothers teachers, pounded African tribal rhythms on drums, over and over. Cars had given way to police bollards and stalls, which lined the main street so that the public need to purchase could be satisfied. The usual purveyors of cultural tat were there: peddlers of crystals and sounds from nature, glow-in-the-dark boiled sweets guaranteed to stain the teeth, and the inevitable dream webs – the adopted totems of a faithless generation. His soul was withdrawing and his vision tightening to the air around him whilst his companion, his lover, considered the wares with a seriousness which their prices suggested but which they did not merit. He sought solace in the architecture, a Dutch gable abutting a Regency façade, the reworkings over centuries of the ideals of living. Above the rooftops cattle grazed in formation left to right across the hill, oblivious to the noise below or the turbulent shatter of the American jets, practising for war above.

Then, amid the ebb and flow of people, they had come to the birds. On perches and tethers low to the ground and close, too close to the crowd, were displayed lithe hawks and falcons, frightened and trapped, owls with their offended, glaring eyes, calmer buzzards, secure perhaps in their size. He watched the people pressing close, like he remembered from zoos, revealing far more of their natures in observing than those who were observed. A young lad, six or eight perhaps, with a round face was waving a long yellow balloon at a tawny owl, who did nothing but turn its head away, blinking yellow eyes, a study of rage. Annoyed by this, the boy leaned forward over the barrier and shouted at the owl, who flapped from his post as far as the jesses would allow. Gap-toothed laughter followed, the mean little pegs stained red by cherryade. His mother poked at him and pulled him back by the shoulder, uncommittedly. The child had one last play and squeezed his pudgy fingers deep into the balloon until it swelled and strained at the extremities before bursting apart and falling, fluid and torn, to the ground. All the birds took to the wing and floundered, constrained; the buzzards shrieked and the merlin stood, wings spread as if injured, panting with its terror. He had watched the lad from the start, sickened and saddened; he seemed immune to the censure of the crowd, insensitive to his mother's embarrassed screaming in his ear. Yet the boy had revealed a truth. Amid the scolds of disapproval and laughter, the flapping of wings and shrieking of raptors, there, from a cage, a raven had watched. She had turned her gaze upon the child for a minute perhaps, cocking her head first one way then another, to consider whether this new element in her world was important. Dismissing it, she resumed her exploration of the cage, her bright intelligence exploring the mesh for weakness, investigating the corners first by sight, then flying up and hanging, probing them with a beak, strong and sharp, before returning to the perch and the search for an escape. He watched this, entranced. She was at least the size of a buzzard but sleeker. Her form was stealth and restraint, a less obvious strength than the onyx talons and scimitar beak of the other. Her blackness was so complete that she almost seemed to have begun before you realised, yet light flickered off her as she twisted and turned. He dreamed of her for months, waking and sleeping, his mind infected by her life. After a while, the attendant had come and hovered near by, noticing his interest and fearful that he might try to release the bird.

'Why is she in a cage and not out with the others?'

'Ravens can untie the knots.'

He nodded and turned away. That night a brawl spilled out from the pub and down the street. Mick the fence lost a tooth.

Now as he watched, a smaller shape left the trees and

mobbed the lower raven, diving and wheeling, driving it out of the thermal and away to the left. From a height its mate must have seen and thundered down, spiralling as if without control until, just above the molester, it appeared to slow without effort, and the powers were reversed. The aggressor retreated and together the ravens began to circle and rise.

'Now there's a thing,' he said out loud.

'What? The cloud?' asked Ben.

'Aye . . . that too. But no, did you see the ravens?'

'The big crows?'

He nodded.

'Why do the other birds always attack them?'

'Fear, I would guess, anger maybe. Just instinct.'

'But they weren't doing anything bad.'

'It doesn't seem to matter.'

They freewheeled the rest of the way and stowed the bikes on the bothy wall. He took the dogs along to the kennels. He did not know how long this would take and getting caught on other business was always a risk.

* * *

The artist was in residence on the front lawn. He stood still, gazing out at the hills beyond the parkland. The paraphernalia of his trade was arranged around him in a C-shape and looked from a distance like a low wall or hedge. To his front was the easel with the canvas pegged unexpectedly high. It did not look like he had painted anything that morning; he had been too distracted by the view.

The gardener approached Michael with genuine interest, partly in the man himself, partly because he was curious how this landscape would be stilled and simplified on to a canvas, and also, inevitably, because of his connection with Lucia. She had surprised him the night before, not by her boldness but by what she seemed prepared to risk. Her troubles too might indicate depths he had not expected though he remained unsure whether this would be a good thing. He was amused by the smock, unmarked as yet by paint and creased crisply down each sleeve, fresh from unpacking. A quaint if sensible choice perhaps; it would turn the breeze which, though light, would soon chill the inactive.

'Good morning. Are you settled?'

'Yes.' Michael's distaste was evident as he considered the gardener again and flicked his hard-edged fringe with a twitch of his head before forcing a smile, 'Thank you.'

'I'd asked the boys to cut the grass this morning.'

'Well, they can't until I've finished!' The residual anger of Michael's previous confrontation flared quickly, raising his colour.

'That's not strictly speaking true. However,' – he raised a hand to stifle Michael's protest – 'I'll find something else for them. Perhaps we could co-ordinate our work to . . .'

'Not possible. I have to paint when the mood and the matter are right. Now look, look at that!' and he jabbed his clean brush with unexpected passion at the view. 'The light is perfect!'

So he looked. And the artist was right; the light and the day were perfection. Thin furls of mist were rising from hollows and the surfaces of the ponds, confusing the boundaries of the worlds of water and air. He breathed it in deeply, feeling the sun upon his face, feeling, for a minute or two, less far away.

Then came Magda, walking into the edge of their vision along the top of the ha-ha wall, her arms outstretched to keep her balance, a creature poised between earth and air. Her black hair flowed in waves to her shoulders and each time she recovered her balance it would crash in disorder over her face and the laughter of her game would come to them, light and clear. She had reached half-way when she saw them and flung an arm high above her head, waving a greeting. He waved back whilst the artist stared; the sun was behind her and shone through the white cotton of her long dress reveal-ing a shadow beneath a veil. She cried out and came running

61

over the grass, bouncing with every third step as if trying to take flight, not slowing at all as she neared so that he had to catch her up and swing her round as she flung her arms around his neck and kissed his cheek with a loud smack. Uninhibited and uncomplicated as she was, Magda's condition, under other dispensations, would have been considered a judgement on her father, Lord Palmer. Here, at least, she was free of that.

'What have you found, Magda?'

'I've been in the orchard, starting to flower, pretty flowers.' She stroked a long, slim finger through the posy of early apple blossom, the round pink buds waiting to burst, the pink and white petals paler, the fresh downy green of new leaf caught up with them.

'Smell.' She held them out for him.

He bent his head to them, closing his eyes to cover the sadness he always felt with Magda; the light, honeyed scent was a joy.

'Were the bees busy?'

'Yes yes, busy bees. Big lazy bees and small shiny bees.' She turned towards Michael and thrust the posy at him. 'Smell . . .'

'Very pretty,' he said distractedly.

She laughed again, throwing out her arms and dropping them so that they slapped against her sides. Two petals were broken and fluttered to the ground, where they settled on her bare foot. She looked at them both smiling, then seemed to notice the canvas. She clambered over the nearest box, to Michael's alarm, then pressed close to him gripping his arm. She shrieked with delight, pointing.

'Oh, there are the trees, lovely trees, and the water, and the dark, dark hills.' It seemed as if she saw these things as her fingers traced their lines upon the blank cloth, her eyes glancing up at the land then back. 'But the sky is too blue, you haven't painted the clouds!' She looked up with confusion in her pale grey eyes at Michael's baffled face.

'There are no clouds,' he managed, though he could not

have looked more uncomfortable had he tried.

'Always clouds,' she said with such seriousness that even she looked sad for a moment. Then she laughed again and jumped out of the ring of boxes and was gone, laughing and running to the Hall, Michael's eyes upon her all the while.

The world seemed drabber without her and the gardener reached for the solace of his tobacco. He half turned to go, then stopped.

'Enjoy it whilst you can. There'll be rain by three.'

He left the artist there and made towards the lads who were stood, hands in pockets, looking bemused next to their redundant mowers.

'I'd get on with some weeding for the rest of the day. When it rains, there are those cuttings to be potted on. I'll be back in tomorrow.'

If they were surprised by this unexpected defeat of their leader, they did not show it. Their smiles and nods seemed to carry other knowledge. Ben was trying hard to look innocent, in a shamefaced way.

'Aye, well. Just get on with it.'

7

Dear Anna,

How are you doing? Well, I hope. I imagine the city's weight is easier to bear at this time of year, despite everything. Have you trained your boss yet?

Thank you for the information regarding our friend. They've been here a month now and his presence has shifted the equilibrium as, I suppose, all new elements must. A funny thing. I've wondered if it is the work rather than the man himself that has been significant. He seems at times determined and at others quite ineffectual, almost as if his spirit ebbs and flows within him. If anything he produces more when ineffectual and weak. In submission to a muse perhaps? Or does that not happen any more? But waxing or waning, he remains a pain in the arse, if you pardon the expression. We are less free to get the work done as we are always upsetting his delicate sensibilities. I would mind less if it looked like they were in proportion to his talent but so far, as you wrote, the efforts have been 'worthy' but not exceptional. It is a difficult place to paint, though, I imagine; it's not just the beauty but the feeling of here. Interestingly, and you might be able to shed some light on this, he has started to paint triptychs – I saw the first one last week. I'd never seen landscapes done like that, for themselves I mean, only incidentally as scenery, like in one of those stylised fifteenth-century pieces we saw in Florence. I like the idea, I must admit; it gives the landscape the right level of importance. And, if I'm fair to him, he's getting better.

His wife has proved an interesting proposition. She ranges more widely than him, always with a camera, always looking for an opportunity, and she's come up with some genuinely interesting takes on the here-and-about. She says she wants to start staff portraits next week. It has been fascinating listening to who wants to be photographed and the reasons they give. I've never heard so many mutual accusations of vanity and you might think she was some sort of goddess, able to bestow greatness, the way people are soliciting her attention. I have the suspicion she won't necessarily do what they expect. I like her more and more as I get to know her.

I'm sorry to be brief. You know how busy it gets at this time of year.

Love as ever,
S

Michael was indeed beginning to paint, after an initial inertia which lasted only a fortnight. An inevitable inertia some might say, on being confronted by the majesty of the land and its overwhelming presence. He felt the hills looming around him and remembered feeling like a child and clinging to the knee of his father in a room full of strangers. There was no father now and, for the first few days of diversionary activity, he reached for a bottle of gin in the morning and Chablis in the afternoon, which set him up for a return to gin prior to supper and the after-dinner malt. The woods which furnished the lower slopes seemed to pulse with life. Their movement infected his mind. When he closed his eyes, the swaying of the canopy in the wind and the imagined sound drove him to distraction.

He dreamed he was a mariner in a wooden boat which yielded and creaked as the waters surged beneath her and the sail whipped full before falling flaccid and useless against the mast where the cord beat, tethered and tormented. Then the ship would be gone and he was lain on his front staring at the stilled waters of the night-time lough, the stars reflecting and enticing so that if he leaned ever so far forward on the cold, smooth rock, he could fashion himself a crown and reaching out, lay claim to a sceptre. Then the dream would change again as he realised he was not above the surface looking down but below it looking up and the water was an oily film before his eyes which blurred the stars, irregular and dull. He opened his mouth to cry out but the brackish water kept him silent. He struck out for the surface but his limbs were caught by something which he could not see and their weight was almost too heavy to bear. And throughout it all, the wind in the trees, like the breathing of a man behind him, raising the hairs on his neck.

Then Lucia would kick him as he writhed around, twisting the covers of their bed on to himself, leaving her cold. He would be awake in the unnatural darkness of this strange country, so that it made no difference if his eyes were open or closed, his heart racing within him, his skin clammy and unshaped. The dreamscape would fade with each beat and the linen of the sheets would become real again. He would reach out a hand and touch Lucia's back, turned towards him, and know her presence.

He would sleep again and sometimes a second dream would recur. A man was stood in dirty clothes facing a fire, so that the man was between Michael and the fire. There was a smell of burning hair and he could see the legs of a small animal, stiff and unnatural, licked by the flames. Nothing was said but he knew that the animal had been shot and killed though he did not know why. As he watched, the man reached for the handle of a pick and beat down upon the body with huge swinging blows, raising both arms high above his head, scattering sparks into the bright morning with each strike, until the end of the haft was bloodied. Then he was being sick, his body convulsing, his hands upon his knees and his eyes upon his feet, and the gardener would turn and smile at him.

After a week he told Lucia of the first dream. She suggested, harshly he thought, that he should drink less. More fairly, she suggested he conquered his fear and did some work, capturing the spirit of the trees and turning it to his will. He did not admit his fear or his fault and he was pleased she did not labour the issue as she might have done at home. After another week he drank only in the evenings and felt, any day now, any day at all, that he could paint. The dreams had ceased leaving only a memory which in time would recede, leaving an impression, a sense.

He sketched and he painted. He found one canvas was insufficient for any view so he chose multiples like stills from a film. Each could make a little sense and impact on their own but when viewed together in threes and fives then some idea of this never-still land could be established. The first triptych he attempted was of an oak in the parkland. He had risen late and it was fully ten by the time he had encamped on the lawn before the house. It appeared to be grass-cutting day again and he wondered just how frequently this happened; it certainly never seemed to get any longer from one day to the next. He was pleased however that when the gardeners saw him standing with his boxes on the path, they signalled – a knuckle to the forehead, a wave of the hand – a willingness to stop and leave the arena to him. He felt quite satisfied and only slightly guilty that on the previous occasion he had failed to produce anything. He mistook their smiles as they wheeled their mowers over the iron lawn-edging and on to the gravel as the beginnings of a rapport. He beamed in return, bouncing slightly on the balls of his feet – a mannerism which Ben would repeat with ridicule later, together with an exaggerated rictus, to the amusement of most.

He set himself up and lit a cigarette, standing tall, his shoulders cast back, his chin raised in defiance of the morning sun. He decided to leave the hills until later and would concentrate on the foreground. He scanned the vista from left to right, hoping to see Magda weaving into view along the ha-ha wall. He did not know where she had been hiding herself in the meantime but he did very much hope to see her soon.

67

He stiffened at the memory of those shoulder blades, lightly tanned and beautifully turned, pointing downwards, leading – no, provoking – the eye into the line of her dress. The firmness of her breasts as she had pressed close to him had lingered in his mind for days and he had sketched a bust of her over and over in his book of working ideas. He glanced downwards involuntarily, and quickly around him to see if anybody was there to see. Nothing had been said regarding Magda, and Michael suspected it would be better if he did not show too much interest. He could not bring himself to consider these thoughts impure in any way – what other purpose did all beauty serve in the world – but he knew from experience that not everybody was as sophisticated as himself.

He would paint the tree in the middle, he decided, the tree with the twisted crown and the branches which did not cross but looked as if they did as they came out from the trunk at what must have been close to the perpendicular before curving up. Overall, it had a rounded top which was even despite the oddity of the interior. The wood was dark as if drawn in charcoal, despite the brightness of the day, and he thought it had very little leaf for this time of year.

He had established a baseline and was considering lateral positioning when the gardener made an appearance. He said his 'Good morning' then stared over Michael's shoulder for what felt like a full five minutes, very disconcertingly, as if expecting a finished picture to appear before his eyes. Just as Michael was going to ask him what type of tree it was, he snorted and wandered away. Michael put him out of his mind and sketched in an outline which brought the tree forward. The green of the sward would form nearly the whole background with only a thin strip of the sky above, as if he were much closer to the tree than was in fact the case and it dominated his vision. Magda appeared and he stammered a 'Hello.' His mind seemed to go to pieces when he saw her; it was like being a teenager again, all blushes and uncertainty. She seemed distant, though, and settled down on one of his boxes, and after an hour or so he had become immune to her quiet little song and the creaking of the lid as she rocked gently. He found it a comforting background noise if anything, a familiar context like the London traffic and a welcome dampener to the mad little birds which kept flitting between the bushes, chirping irritatingly.

He moved the tree forward so that it was the singular focus of the picture, but as he painted it a strange transformation took place. His distance from the tree was such that he could not discern the texture or indeed colour of the bark. The painted tree developed *primivitised*, like the work of a sophisticated child who has not quite grasped representation. Initially he was unhappy and mixed fresh oils to overwork it but as he raised the primed brush Magda broke off from her song,

'No.'

'No?'

'Good as it is. Now colour the leaves.'

He looked again, first at his canvas then at the park, and wondered that she might have known his intention. He lit his last cigarette, scrunching the packet and jamming it into the pouch on the front of his smock, narrowing his eyes to consider the colours of the corolla of leaves which, as yet, were just bursting bud. Only when he had mixed the appropriate tints to capture the coppered green of the new life did Magda resume her song.

He worked quickly and even surprised himself, so that by lunchtime, for him at least with the clock striking one, it was mostly finished. The only naked canvas was the thin strip of sky, which looked now like a blanket of snow about to descend. He could not resist his hunger any longer, there seemed to be something in the air here, he had never been so hungry before, but he did not mind unduly as, if anything, he had started to lose some weight.

Lunch was a slightly strange soup of small green beans, barley and Savoy cabbage awash in a clear, thin liquor. His heart sank at the prospect. The cook fixed him with a look when she saw his dismay and he felt immediately ungrateful and trivial. She was a tall, elegant lady who carried herself like a dancer; she flowed in and out of the kitchen, her movement too fluid to be a walk. Her voice was a rich contralto, the depths of which he knew he would never know, and her speech verged on the languid. She must have been a terrifying and proud beauty in her youth but age had mellowed that; experience a patina which made her more and less attractive. Still, she was like the ripest fruit on the branch, for picking just before it turns or falls.

He smiled ruefully and said thank you before taking a seat at the end of one of the benches, within easy reach of a basket of coarse-grained bread. To his surprise the soup was good, peppery and seasoned with elusive herbs, and with only two slices of the still-warm bread, he felt well filled. He returned his bowl and plate and poured himself a coffee from the pot which sat on the coffee machine. It was the last cup in the jug and about an hour old but it still tasted good. He tipped in a spoonful of demerara, which crept and crumbled, not that he took sugar usually but it looked so appealing. He returned to his seat and began to wonder for the first time at the level of provision these servants, as he thought of them, enjoyed. He was alone in the refectory, so he took a good look around. The floor was stone but nicely finished and the room did not feel demeaned by the absence of a carpet. He could see the sense of it, here and there angles of mud had been shed from the cleats of dirty boots, although the scrapers and brushes at the exterior door looked well used. The boards were of dark oak, long and thick, and were polished deeply after so many years of use. They were unmarked by the casual vandalism of communal property; there were no nicks along the edges where bored diners had toyed with their knives, no names or initials to personalise or lay claim to a place at them. The walls were rough-plastered and whitewashed, but this simplicity

emphasised the beauty of the tables. A large fireplace dominated one end but it was clear it had not been lit for some
time. It would provide a generous heat when burning and he
had a warming image of workers coming in from the cold of
winter and congregating in the space in front of it. Two pictures hung on the wall and he did not need to go closer to
know that they were originals and very good. He wondered
if those who ate here every day ever looked at them or
whether they had become wallpaper. He suspected they
might; there was a difference to the people here that he was
struggling to identify. He pushed his finger idly through the
ring of spilt coffee, making moist patterns on the dark wood.
The coffee seemed colourless in comparison. He wanted to
use the word 'dignity' but it seemed too static, and 'noble'
was just wrong. They were differently focused for certain,
maybe even a touch Zen. He finished his drink and went out,
pausing as he did so to say thank you again and to apologise
for spilling coffee.

Magda had flown and was nowhere to be seen, and for a
moment he was sad to have lost his shadow. He had become
used to her being around and was amazed that he could concentrate so well when she was there; he had never been good
at working in company. Lucia's presence drove him to distraction, which reminded him that he had not seen her
around all day. They had snapped at each other over toast in
the kitchen that morning – the two seemed to go together
these days. He put her from his mind and considered his canvas, remaining very pleased and feeling that he had managed
to capture something of the light and of the lightness of those
leaves, so at odds with the solidity of the tree as if they were
a mist forming on the top of a hill, a thing separate but
caused. The light had changed and now dusty black clouds
were marching in ranks towards him. The sky behind was
brilliant still and he worked quickly to capture the moment.
He was just finishing as the first heavy drops of rain began to

71

fall and he grabbed the canvas and ran at full tilt to the Hall to shelter in the rear porch. He stowed it against the wall and returned to recover the rest of his kit. Lightning flashed in the quick-darkening sky and was followed swiftly by the shatter of thunder. There would be no more work that day and he stood in the porch with his shirt sticking to his skin, shivering now and then, as he watched the pelting rain. The hills had disappeared and the world had contracted to the park around the house. He could still see his tree through the sheets of water which were falling around it and he was loving the play of the lightning, which seemed to illuminate the mist, piercing it with moments of visibility, revealing the cattle in the far fields and here and there a stand of trees. A figure was running – no, dancing – across the park and although he could not be sure, he thought it must be Magda caught up in her beautiful madness.

He smiled and turned his attention to his work. It was an oddity, there was no doubt. The light of the land and the light of the sky did not belong in the same composition and yet this contradiction gave a sense of time and development to what could have been a very static subject. Looking at it he felt an emotion with which he had become unacquainted – satisfaction – and he decided that this place was not as unnerving as he had at first thought.

* * *

Lucia had spent the morning on her back in the maze. Ever since her first visit she had been meaning to return to it and she was not disappointed. The manipulation of her spatial sense was as acute as she remembered and she wanted to commit something of this to film. She had wandered in it for a while, wondering again at the complexity achieved by such simple elements, the pale gravel, the dark hedges, the bright sky, and here and there, a white statue, sharp and distinct against the yew, familiar in form but strangely alien and, when considered, not really required. Simple forms would be better, obelisks or pillars, or even abstracts. Eventually she had reached the Cloister, although that had not been her intention, and she smiled to herself as she lay on the star table and looked up at the square of sky, so neatly framed. The stone was smooth and warm and this seemed like a good place to begin. She pitched herself this way and that, hanging her head down over the edge so that her hair tumbled and fell like golden light to the ground. She took pictures of the 'roof' where it met the sky, varying the proportions of each, frame by frame, working from straight sections to corners, covering all aspects to compare the light. She moved from the table and lay under the 'walls', leaning in and out to create similar variations of hedge and sky. Then on to the damp grass in the corners, which penetrated her shirt and cooled her. She shot the apex, the walls looming out and above, leaving a wedge of pallid blue. She had chosen a good film to leave some colour and texture in the yew and the final prints were vertiginous and disorientating just as she had desired.

Eventually she had tired of shuffling on her back to get the right frame; the gravel had dug into her and left her sore. The claustrophobia of the maze was starting to oppress her spirit and she felt she had done all she could for one day. She had walked home, as she thought of it, more easily now, to change cameras and collect more films. She had planned to wander in the park to see if anything caught her eye and if her feet took her to the gardener's lodge by five o'clock, as they had done every day, so be it.

They had come to an arrangement, the pair of them. More accurately, he had asked her not to appear before five so that he had time to 'turn around' – feeding the dogs, preparing a dinner, eating something small to tide him over. He needed a certain order if his life were to run smoothly; there were too many things in his environment which could get out of hand if neglected. She had started to need the contact, her body expected it and she found herself getting restless as the time approached. Some afternoons she could not keep it from her mind and would struggle on trying to work, or else give up and luxuriate in the thought of it. The slight delay he had requested was not a refusal but had heightened her erotic expectation just as effectively. She was not used to being told no.

She had eaten a slice of bread in the kitchen and restocked her equipment, including some monochromes in case she could persuade him to work with her. She was fascinated by the sinews behind his knees and the hollows which were created there as he walked across the room. The muscle on his flank at the base of his ribs similarly intrigued and she never tired of tracing it with her fingers, moving downwards off the hardness of the ribcage on to the softer flesh. Then she would ask him to tense and she would press at it firmly, then release, examining the white pressure marks surrounded by red. Sometimes he sat up to stoke the fire, his back to her. The muscles of his shoulders would ripple under tight skin, casting shadows. She would appraise him as if he were an animal at market and she a butcher. She had worked with talented models before, models whose dedication could not be questioned, whose denial and self-discipline had made them well-defined, godlike specimens of male flesh. But there had always been a pointlessness about it, a disconnectedness from purpose. Here she had found an example whose very purpose had sculpted him. She felt the restraint in his hands when he held her, such strong hands, and she remembered the look of sadness in his eyes after the hare. She had not told him what she wanted to photograph, he had not really allowed the discussion and his refusal did not leave room for a why. But if she could convince him of the depersonalising direction of her work, he might acquiesce. It would be worth the attempt.

She was so engaged with her scheme that she did not notice the state of the sky as she left the house. She was well across the park when the rains started, sudden large drops which soaked her instantly. Then came the thunder and with it an urge to run, not with any thought to escape, just to feel fast. She had watched the Clydesdales in the paddock the day before, careering up and down, tossing their heads and shaking the earth, revelling in their own strength and the warmth of the sun upon their backs. She started to laugh at the daftness of so much water in the sky and her running turned to dancing as she abandoned any intention to work and made instead for the lodge.

The day was prematurely dark and she lit the lantern as she entered, standing long enough for a puddle to form around her feet. She dripped through to the kitchen and embraced the range, trying to recover some warmth. She stoked it as she had learnt and stripped off her sodden clothes, hanging them along the towel rail, before putting a small pan of water on to boil for a hot toddy. She found a woollen rug in the front room and wrapped herself in it until the water boiled. She had already put a teaspoon of honey in a glass and dissolved it with a charge of whiskey. There was half a lemon face down on a plate on the table and she cut a slice from this, studding it with cloves, and dropping it in. The smell was almost enough on its own to warm her but she settled herself with her back to the oven, cupping the glass to revive her hands, and lingering there until she felt restored.

It was early still, despite the deception of the light, and the thought of a bath and some dry clothes started to overwhelm her. Enough had passed between them for her to be sure he would not mind, so for the first time she ventured upstairs.

The bare boards creaked beneath her feet but at least felt warmer than the stone flags. She found the bathroom and smiled inwardly; it had the same mixture of simplicity and opulence that she had seen downstairs. An expensive shaving soap sat on a shelf above the sink and she lifted the lid and smelt it, recognising the notes from the man himself. The razor had a lacquered handle, and was open, the long blade revealed and unarguable. She touched it tentatively as if to connect with the face which it caressed every day. Seeing these things redundant in this empty house filled her with sadness as if their owner might be dead and never returning, and they would sit there, each in their space, untouched for ever. The dark tan strop which hung by the sink was more reassuring, it felt warm and bore the marks of use, unlike the clinical inertness of the razor. She sipped her drink and moved on. Behind the door hung a short robe of dark brushed cotton. She exchanged her rug for it and felt comforted and connected by the now familiar scent. The bath was original and immense and she wondered as she turned the tap whether there would be enough water in the tank to fill more than a small fraction of it. A handful of salts from the Delft jar perfumed the now steaming water with a memory of spices and the hot days of summer. Lucia sat on the edge and began to sing.

8

His annoyance flashed as he realised she was there before him. Tired and sodden-clothed as he was from the walk back, he had wanted nothing more than a quiet soak in the bath; a good half-hour until the heat had penetrated his joints.

He put his hand to her clothes and, as they were dry, he removed them and despite himself, folded them neatly and placed them on a chair. He fed the range and steamed next to it with the door open until his jeans became uncomfortable, rubbing them to spread the heat. He collected the dogs' food and put them out in the yard where they would be happier in the thunder. They had stood quaking with fear since entering the house, not even bothering to shake themselves dry, which was one benefit of the storm at least.

He stripped off his outer layers and laid them over the top of the oven to dry quickly, wrapping a towel around his waist to save himself the trip upstairs. He wandered over to the sink and leaned against that, considering the rain that beat against the window, disrupting the sheets of water flowing there already. The gutter he had been meaning to fix since the autumn was overflowing in a cascade which divided his view. The apparent chaos of its fall caught the lightning and for a while it seemed to hypnotise him. Eventually he stirred, made coffee and rolled, and sank into other reveries which did not seem to have either a beginning or an end. They were there always, it seemed, when he stopped, the memories he wished he no longer had, his own personal spectre – as faithful as his shadow.

A true darkness was forming behind the cloud. He washed his hands and padded through to the pantry, his feet now so numb with the cold of the floor that he had ceased to feel their discomfort. He reached down the poult which he had killed, drawn, and plucked the day before and returning to the kitchen, slapped it down on the woodblock, extricating the hanging hook and laying it aside for washing. He removed the feet and wing tips, crunching through the joints with firm movements of the cleaver. As he manipulated the body the eyelid eased open as the head rolled from side to side. He took it off with distaste, casting it with the feet into the fire. It was an easier proposition without the soulless eye considering him and the voiceless mouth accusing. The neck he skinned and placed in a pan of water with the wing tips and the other raw ingredients for a stock. Tomorrow would be soup. Today was not yet decided and he poked at the bird, considering its potential. Finally he split it down the middle of the breastbone, forcing down his weight through the edge of the blade with both hands. He seasoned flour, coating all the surfaces of the pieces and dusting the excess from them. Whilst the meat sealed and turned golden in the butter, he chopped leek and diced carrot, taking time to do it properly, getting absorbed by the task. He lifted out the chicken and transferred the pan to the cooler plate to sweat the vegetables gently for a few minutes until they glistened in the fat and their aroma filled the room.

He uncorked the bottle of white wine he had collected from the cellar on his way home. It was a golden, buttery Chardonnay which tumbled into the glass with the light and life of mountain streams. He sipped at it, nodding in appreciation and rotating the bottle to examine the label; a woodcut of a château with a pale horse in the foreground. Swiss. He would remember it and request another. He replaced the chicken and poured a generous quantity of the wine over it until the vegetables were half submerged. He sprinkled pearl barley around the edge and added more bay leaves, fresh from the garden, and thyme. The pot began to bubble, slowly at first then quicker, and he covered it, transferring it to the oven, his anger forgotten. He poured himself a second glass and, leaving the bottle, went to find her.

Lucia had languished in the bath until the heat of the water and the balm of the toddy had filled her so completely with drowsiness that she feared slipping under the water, asleep and unknowing. She extricated herself and dried off with the rough towel which hung over a warming rail, trying to wake up but enjoying the subdued feeling of pressing sleep also.

She went in pursuit of clothing but the first door she opened revealed a bare room, the far reaches of which resisted the light from the lamp she held out before her. The storm raged outside, lashing the windows with sharp rain, so hard it sounded like hail. The lightning threw up shadows, revealing an empty hearth and, in a corner, a wooden box like an old tea chest. She shivered as the darkness reclaimed them and the pool of light retreated like a wave, back along the broad wooden boards towards her. There was no need to go further and she turned to another door. At first she thought that this room was empty too, before she spied the corner of the bed behind the door. Encouraged, she walked forward, holding the lamp up until a chest of drawers and a wardrobe were revealed, each flanking another fireplace. She set the lamp on the mantel and opened the wardrobe. It contained very little, but a shirt was there, suspended in space and swaying slightly from the pull of the disturbed air. She lifted this down and pulled it over her head, pressing the cool cloth down along her arms and against her body in an attempt to warm it. Two pairs of shoes, one brown and one black, were all that occupied the rail at the bottom and again, she felt a twinge of sadness seeing the polish overlaid with dust, as if they were relics, never to be worn again. She shut them away and shook her head, biting at her lip and wondering at herself. They were just shoes after all. But there was something about the way this house was occupied; there it was, yes, occupied not lived in, a permanent temporariness which disturbed her and made her even more curious about this man who brought her so much pleasure. She investigated the drawers, looking for something for her lower half. The first one she tried was empty except for a smell of wood and wax and a mustiness of forgotten herbs which seemed more acute in the gloom. The second felt equally light as she pulled it open but the light from the lamp caught on something in the void. She reached in a hand and retrieved a photograph.

She took the lamp over to the window to make the most of the combined lights. On a headland stood two young men, one of whom she recognised. The angle was such that both the cliffs and the sea could be seen behind them, and with the strange way in which the land tumbled away, it appeared as if they were somehow caught ungrounded. It was a bad composition – a throwaway image like most photos – but it caught a certain cheerfulness and revealed much accidentally. There was a midsummer sky with fluffed white clouds and shiny blurs she assumed were seagulls. The land was a rich green, and here and there were bright splashes of yellow gorse. The figures were small in comparison with the drama of the landscape and the photographer had cut them off below their waists. With the easy ways of the young, each had an arm cast over the other's shoulder as if to display an untroubled friendship for the benefit of the taker, whom she thought now must be a woman. Their dissembling was not complete, though, and she could see from the way each carried his weight that one was happier with the closeness than the other. They looked – and she considered this for some time, angling the picture in the light as if it made a difference – as if they had suffered some event and that event, whilst not forgotten, had started to lose its power as if its memory was insufficient to compete with the natural beauty behind. Their eyes held shadows which belied their smiles. Both were lean and fit-looking, and tanned a golden brown – the tan of a temperate sun – and so very, very young. Instinctively she turned it over; a place name which meant nothing and a date, twelve years past. She frowned at it and turned it back over, examining the face she knew, wondering just how old he was.

A wave of guilt at her prying swept over her and she

replaced the picture. She checked the other drawers but could not find anything for her legs and now she did not wish to delve too deeply in the layers of clothes. Intrigued and confused in equal measure, she wandered over to the narrow bed. Setting the lamp on the bedside table next to a portrait of a woman – also young, also attractive – in a silver frame, she climbed in. The linen sheets were cold against her bare legs and she tucked her knees up under her chin, drawing the blankets up around herself for warmth and binding her shins with her arms in just the same way as he had found her on the first night. She was missing something in that picture; such a strange image to find in a house almost devoid of images. Dark eyes stared at her from the table until she could bear them no longer and turned the frame away.

He had heard no movement and presumed she must be asleep. He peered round his bedroom door, the light he carried falling across the raised mound of her body and revealing a face, sleeping soundly. He placed the lamp down by his feet and leaned himself against the wall, watching her in the diminished light. She was more peaceful than he had seen her, and an urge to smooth her tousled hair, strewn over the pillow, back and away from her face, wrestled with the knowing that this would wake her, destroying the sweetness beyond recovery. Now and then her brows would knit and her mouth purse, or the lips would move as if in silent prayer. He cast his eyes to the floor as if intruding on a precious thing he had no right to see, then he looked around the room. The shutters were open and the curtains undrawn, and a shaft of silver moonlight shone through, illuminating the floor. The far reaches of the room were denied to him and he gave them no time. Turning back to Lucia, he thought that she had not meant to sleep. The lamp was dark beside the bed but he knew it was low in paraffin, he had been meaning to fill it all week. He left her sleeping and feeling less agitated returned downstairs, collecting clean, dry trousers on the way.

He lit the fire, which thankfully did not put up any resistance despite the heavy air, dense with water. His mind was with her peace, she seemed so belonging there that he had not wished to disturb her, nor, he thought, to encourage her to do it again. He poked at the wood for no reason other than to move it around, and pottered through to check the progress of the casserole. He pricked the chicken with a fork, the juices still pink, and reached for the wine as a substitute for the energy he craved. An owl shrieked in the night and he clattered the bottle back on to the sideboard, edgily. He cast around for something to bolster his reserves through the half-hour before the meal would be ready. He collected the book he was reading and returned to his chair by the fire, where it sat redundantly in his lap, his thumb parting the leaves, as he stared into the growing flames.

He did not know whether he had slept or stayed awake, but he was aware the storm was over and the night still, wrapped coolly around the house. He roused himself, placing another log upon the fire, rising and stretching, clicking out his back as he did so. The food smelled good and he lifted out the pot, raising the lid and testing the meat again, needlessly, as it was breaking apart in the turmoil of the simmering liquid. The barley had plumped satisfyingly and half a smile broke across his face in anticipation. He let the dogs back in and they seemed grateful, circling the table and snuffling the air before settling at the foot of the range and licking off their coats, their tongues breaking between the pads of their feet. They were good friends and he hunkered down and gave them both a stroke, their tails beating the floor in appreciation.

Sighing, he raised himself and rinsed off his hands under the tap; their coats were gritty from the bouncing rain. He should wake Lucia. He did not know what explanation she had given Michael for her absence in the early evening but it was no longer early evening and the excuse may have expired.

She had turned in her sleep and was on her back, her hair spread over the pillow in a crumpled halo. He sat on the edge of the bed and cradled her face with the whole of a hand. She turned into its pressure and warmth with a trust he found difficult. He did not wish to break her sleep but he did so and she opened her eyes, blinking slightly, and kissed the palm of his hand, raising her own to press his into her lips. He felt it in his spine and closed his own eyes in case she saw.

He had climbed in behind her and they sat for some time, his arms around her, her weight against him, in the gentle darkness. They spoke hardly at all. Every so often he held her more tightly before releasing her, or stroked the hair from her face, feeling it smooth under his callused hand. Every so often she clenched her hands around his or raised one and kissed it noiselessly. It was fine, blithe, to be so near to someone again, near without questions or explanations, just the physical knowing of another. The strangeness of an old peace was settling itself unexpectedly in his heart, walking twice around in circles, scratching up the rug for a bed, not minding the dust which rose from it.

'Who's in the picture?' she asked after a while.

'Anna . . . My wife.'

She shifted her weight and glanced upwards and backwards at him.

'I'm sorry.'

'For what?'

Lucia's confusion swept her face and she wondered that he could be so cold. With some effort she fractured the pause.

'Well, she's never been here, has she? I mean, this is your house; the single bed, the clothes, the furnishings. A woman has never lived here. I thought perhaps she was dead.'

'No. She lives in London.'

She turned fully in the bed, holding his face in her hands and lifting the chin which was descending to his chest. She held his eyes for as long as she was able, trying to discern some emotion. He felt the warmth of her touch and her need

83

to understand and he closed himself to her, returning her gaze with eyes devoid of feeling.

'My God, what happened to you?' She turned from him and leaned forward in the bed, and although he could not be certain, he thought she might be crying. The unspoken wrapped around them, insulating each in a world of solitary thought. Eventually he half sighed and half breathed deeply; he did not have time for such luxuries.

'I've cooked a meal if you would like some. Then I'll run you back.'

They ate together, he somewhat mechanically, she aware of the pleasures the flavours and textures would have given her in any other circumstance. Sally and Phlebus sat each side of him, resting chins upon his thighs with imploring eyes. Every so often he would lower a hand and stroke them. The food was good, hearty, but her questions about the recipe met with a minimal response until she realised at last it was of no interest to him, and she gave up.

It was their first night of abstinence and she was not sure whether a bond had been broken or whether a new one was being formed. That sudden lack of ease which rose between them for the first time left her feeling subdued. She breathed deeply, pressing her back against the front door, wondering if she was being reasonable. This was turning out differently to how she had expected. The price she would pay for her pleasure, perhaps, that he would keep her at arms' length. He must have grown used to being on his own; he must have forgotten the words and what was expected, burned by his separation, no doubt. There was time.

She lingered in the hall of the Dower considering the moisture rising up her trousers from her ankles and wondering if they were convincing when Michael appeared, suitably drunk.

'I looked for you but couldn't find you anywhere.'

'I was developing in the cellar. It seems to have rained.'

'Yes . . . yes, most of the afternoon.' He hoped he had not responded to the lie. 'I'd finished a picture just before it began. Come and see.'

Reluctantly she followed him through, appraising the studio, prepared to be annoyed. He placed it against the wall for her and she crouched down to consider it more closely. She could hear him shifting from foot to foot behind her, waiting for a judgement. It pleased her quite genuinely – it showed some imagination – and she was reminded of the Michael she fell in love with those years ago.

'It's quite small. Did it take you long?'

'I worked quite quickly. And I ate some lunch.' His shoulders sagged as he spoke and she had a twist of remorse.

'I like it.' She stood, patting his arm and kissing his cheek, leaning into him and lowering her eyes provocatively.

9

Michael's confidence was growing day by day, as if nurtured by the warmth of the late spring sun and the intermittent rain which refreshed the growth, washing out the sky, leaving it gleaming. He had finished his oaken triptych within a week. The 'second' day, as it might have been, was abandoned. He had made much too late a start to paint the tree in the early light after the predictable consumption of the night before and the unexpected Lucia, and the rains had come early and there was, of course, that nice bottle over lunch which had seduced him so effectively. Ultimately it was fortuitous. He had taken a walk over to the Hall in the late afternoon, getting thoroughly soaked to the knees in the process from the long, wet pasture, and hung about on the lawn, looking out and considering his tree, enjoying the solitude of the garden and realising, for the first time, that he had rarely been alone since coming here. Always, now when he thought about it, there had been someone coming or going, and he had the sudden and disturbing thought that he had been 'kept an eye on'. He turned quickly and scanned the Hall from top to bottom but the windows stared back blankly; most of them were shuttered anyway. He looked to the left and right to see if anybody had seen this odd action but truly he was alone. He relaxed again, smiling slightly at his nascent paranoia and returned to the oak.

The deep golden light of evening was drawing out the red tints of the leaves, which already were fuller and better set than the previous day, swollen by the rain. The lesser angle of the light revealed more colour in the bark also, at least along the edge where it struck, if something roughly circular could have an edge.

So it was that he was there the day after, painting in the gentle warmth of late afternoon. He had spent the earlier part of the day plotting points on a fresh canvas, as a structure to follow, a proportion. He thought this would emphasise the similarity and the difference of the pictures. He had been struck by something he had read once, though he could not remember who had said or written it, some Roman or other: You never step into the same river twice. Nonsense, obviously, unless you are going to split hairs about the meaning of river, but an interesting thought all the same. Now, as he looked at his pictures of the oak, one in morning, one midday, one in evening, it was definitely the same tree. And yet, and yet it looked so different. The changes had been there over the week, in the coming into leaf and during the day, with the angle and intensity of the light. In one sense he had three pictures each capturing different times of day and in another he had one representation split in three encompassing simultaneously all times of day.

He was so pleased with them that he hung them in the Dower as an inspiration to work well. It was there that the gardener saw them when he came to relight the range and after moments of silent looking asked him, 'Where is the birdsong?' and then, most curiously, had stated, in a such a way that to disagree would seem unreasonable, that they were in the wrong order; evening should be first, then morning, then midday. Michael had looked suitably disdaining, or so he thought – the gardener had presumed trapped wind – but later he had tried it for a week or so. It was a strange thing because it did look better, but he could not overcome his desire for the 'proper' progression, however dissatisfied the reversion left him feeling.

An odd proposition, that gardener, he decided. He had always seemed so self-contained. There was a minimum interchange; he, the gardener, being forthcoming enough not to be considered rude but enough perhaps to be impolite.

Then, when he had finished the third picture, it was late morning and he fancied some coffee before tidying away, he was putting his hand to the heavy wooden door of the under-croft when he glanced through the window at its side. Two people, a man and a woman, were sat with their backs to him, close together like lovers. The man had to be the gardener, he had seen him earlier that day and recognised the dark plaid shirt, but oddly both his hands were embedded deeply into the thick hair at the back of his head, his face cast downwards and his shoulders hunched as if he were in crisis. The woman was sat turned into him, very erect, and one hand was resting in the middle of his back with the weight of years. He stood on the outside, his foot still on its heel, perplexed and looking in. Magda joined them, setting a glass of water down and hovering, shifting her weight from foot to foot. A wave of envy swept him as he witnessed their complicity and he for-got his coffee. The cook raised her head and must have spoken; Magda nodded and sat, glancing towards him as she did so. He froze, unblinking; Magda's urgent mouthing across the table, her finger raised to point, the turning heads. Too late he wheeled from the door, the gravel announcing his retreat. He wondered what secrets he had been disturbing.

With his confidence growing, Michael began to explore the areas of the demesne further from the house, as a fledgling would as it finds its wings. He painted more oaks, always in entirety, including the ruined stump of one he found like a broken tooth, the ruptured surface a pale enamel, the bark a spreading stain of blood. He discovered the bluebell wood of hazel coppice and birch and he found as he walked among them, trying not to damage the flower spikes, that he was developing a passion for these trees. He wanted to paint all their aspects rather than consider the wider landscape. His first hazel series picked out a single, multi-stemmed stooling about four years old. The straight, shining rods fascinated him. Their apparent regularity of form, as if manufactured, and of colour, like the sheen of mercury, although closer inspection revealed a more complex toning than he had at first thought. It drew him time and again. He would stroke them and feel them, cold to his touch, and peer at them, wondering at all the little holes in the bark and at his ignorance of these before.

When the Dower had been furnished, somebody had thoughtfully included a changing screen. He had presumed at first that this was some sort of primitive joke. Later he thought it may have been well-intentioned ignorance, expecting him to be requiring models and wishing to preserve their modesty. It gave him an idea, though, and he carried it over to Jack's workshop to see if he could knock up five frames of equal proportion. He had bumped into Lucia on the way, who seeing the screen had looked askance at him before dryly inquiring if he was going swimming. She had been blowing hot and cold, though, of late.

He painted the hazel on the five panels Jack had prepared. He had been aghast when he realised Jack had misunderstood, then delighted, shaking Jack's hand and asking at least three times what type of wood they were and how many more he could have. Jack had shrugged and led him through to the store. 'Plenty' had been his final verdict then, when Michael showed no signs of leaving. 'But I think you'll find that one is the best grain for painting over. Just let me know how you get on with it,' before ushering him out with his trophies.

He etiolated the leaf-free parts of the stems and filled the whole length of the panels with them. The background was simplified grass in light and shade with here and there a bluebell, rather than the carpet of reality which he thought would distract attention from the bark. When he was done he took them back to Jack, who hinged them for him so that they could be arranged concavely or convexly, or even positioned as a pentagon to be walked around. 'A bonny tree, the hazel' had been Jack's comment, but Magda clapped and laughed very satisfyingly. Lucia expressed surprise at the novelty and he thought she was piqued. He assured her that he was not stealing her thunder.

Lucia was photographing the cook that day and reduced her to a mouth, her eyes and her left cheekbone. This too would be a three-part study. Elsie had not wished to be taken but Lord Palmer had asked her specifically. Inevitably she was impatient and severe; there was work to be done and she was not at all sure about this girl. Could any truth be captured by the fraction of a second exposure of her lens and film, any truth of value? She had her doubts. She gave up her time all the same and was intrigued to see the result.

Lucia was not at all sure either. Elsie was the first female member of staff she had tackled and was immune to the usual flirtation. She had wanted Elsie stripped to the waist but the refusal had been intractable and she had settled for what she could. Elsie's eyes were cold like few she had seen before, as if her soul were far away. Lucia considered this through her viewfinder, firing off shots to fill the silence with the clicking report, a substitute for words. The soul was there, oh so painfully present and alive, but refused, veiled from the unwelcome voyeur. She was looking into the eyes of the gardener, her lover, and the similarity left her choked and confused. The questions she wanted to ask died on her tongue and she finished the session as early as was decent – not wanting the physical closeness the process required – and sank down on to the bench, pressing her back into the cool plaster of the wall and staring at the picture of a hare on the wall opposite. At first she did not realise it was dead – it was laid as if running at full stretch. The tones were dark and the stain of the wound at first looked just like the natural colouring of the animal, a shadow behind the shoulder. The eyes, though, were half closed and had an unnatural opacity. It was a morbid subject under which to eat dinner and she was surprised it had been tolerated, no matter how good it was. She despaired of Michael ever painting anything to match it and she wondered, not for the first time, just what she had done.

Through in the kitchen the cook had resumed her duties with an unexpected clattering of pans which shook Lucia from her reverie. She had never before questioned that the people she met wanted her approval and she wielded this scythe with a confidence which in most situations made it true. As for the people here, well, their lives were organised towards an end which lay beyond her approval or disapproval. These things should mean nothing to her but in fact she was wrong-footed by them. Even some of the younger men had seemed indulgent towards her, seeing her game for what it was. The thought that she might need the love of these people disturbed her. It was time to go home. A fortnight or three weeks, perhaps a month, no point going for less, but if she didn't go now, she thought, she would go mad. Her reactions had had an edge to them recently, a nervousness which she did not enjoy. At home, at least, she knew the rules.

* * *

It had been only three days before the itch grew too great and had needed scratching. She had tracked him down, ignoring the half-smiles of the gardeners she asked, in a small, walled garden. It was a claustrophobic place with luxuriant climbers on the high walls, reducing the space further. Trusses of buds hung like grapes from them, ovoid and plump, soon to be purple. He was weeding between the swollen rhizomes of irises, fat upon the surface of the soil and somewhat repugnant. The sharp tool cut through the tilth and she watched him as he worked; he had smiled and said hello but not stopped. She was amazed he did not carve up the plants as he went. She added the sinews at the base of his neck and his knuckles to her mental list, sitting on a cool stone bench whilst she waited for him.

The week which followed had conformed to the pattern. She had sought him out and disrupted his work, one day inspecting the new spears of asparagus, another planting out *Salvia involucrata* in the family LABIATAE, or so he told her, not that it meant much, firming it into the soil with ungloved hands. Their love-making had been brutal, acrimonious almost, despite his silence. Now as she sat, disturbed by her session, she wanted to return to his lodge and she ran the tip of her tongue over the edge of her teeth in contemplation. She wanted him without risk. She wanted to see the picture again, hoping that it might hold a clue which would help her to understand. Her mind was set and she would make no apology.

He did not get angry this time when he returned. He had been wanting to see her properly before the trip she had talked of; he felt perhaps that he had not been fair recently. She was still in the bath and he soaped her back, pushing his fingertips hard into the muscle so that she flinched and twisted but asked him to carry on, feeling the knots loosen. He shaved whilst she finished and, towelled off, she sat on the edge of the bath watching him raise the shaving bowl and froth it with the swift movements of the brush, applying the thickened soap over his chin. He had replaced the bowl and brush and dipped his hands to rinse them before lifting the razor. He caught her smile in the mirror as he reached for the strop, gliding the blade up and down it with long movements, smiling in return. She listened to the dry rasp as the bristle cut and smiled again as the face she knew was revealed strip by strip with the attentions of the razor. She was thinking on to other photographs she could take.

'Could you run more water in? There should be plenty.'

She obliged and he returned to finish his work. When he was done she rose and kissed him, smelling the fresh soap and the coolness of his face. He dried the razor carefully and placed it back on the shelf, rinsing the sink with swirling hands of cold water.

She returned the favour, feeling his back unyielding beneath her hands but he made appreciative noises. It was a reciprocation which restored much between them.

* * *

'How long will you be gone for?' he asked. She felt the vibrations in his chest, her head resting in the crook of his shoulder. They were warm and becalmed, and really she did not wish to think about it.

'Two, three weeks perhaps. Will you miss me?' she toyed.

He shrugged, dislodging her head, but followed it with a wink and a smile.

'Sod.' She turned in mock hurt, resting her back against him. The hurt became real to her as the moments passed and he did not ask further. 'I've some meetings to go to about the work here. And a friend is due any time now, her first, I'd like to be there,' she volunteered, knowing she was giving herself away, her tone too eager and determined. She turned her head, scanning the room as she sought to engage his interest. 'You never mentioned that you played guitar,' she asked in surprise, seeing the instrument he had propped in the corner, meaning to return it to under the bed before she came round.

'I played guitar.' And he held his hand out before her face, the thickened, curving fingers malformed by the labour, the skin cracked and ingrained with dirt, nails worn down by use. She took it and kissed it, lingering with it there against her mouth.

'A pity.'

'Perhaps. Some consequences are unforeseen, aren't they?' But his voice was heavier than his words and she discerned regret in it.

'Would you mind if I . . .?'

'Not at all. Please.' A little too quickly.

She retrieved the guitar and perched at the foot of the bed, half-turned towards him. She smiled at him but he could see that her attention was already with the instrument. She stroked her hand flat over the rosewood, feeling the patina of age, before cupping her fingers around the rear of the neck and slid-

93

ing up the smoothed cedar. She enclosed it, judging the balance and finding it perfect, adjusting her weight to suit it.

'It has a lovely tone.'

'I've tried to keep her sweet.'

She tuned it to her liking, cocking her head as she did so, her hair falling on to its shoulder so that she had to toss back her head like a horse to clear it. It was not far out and she began to feel her way around it until seamlessly, a tune began to emerge, her fingers remembering of their own accord. She smiled again as she recognised the piece and embraced it. She was playing an enchantment for herself as one tune grew into another as she followed some unconscious narrative.

The racking sob from the other end of the bed broke her concentration. She stopped and looked around, and carried on looking in shock, her fingers hovering above the strings. He was hunched forward, one hand over his eyes, the other enclosing his ribs, as if trying to hold back wave after wave of the tears that shook and battered him uncontrollably. Hastily laying the instrument aside she clambered up on the bed, kneeling before him and drawing him into her. He did not embrace her but stayed wrapped, riding the storm of grief which swept over him. She was reeling as she held him, her arms doing nothing to still the sobs, so that her body was moved also. At times he would be quiet and she would hush consolations she did not realise she knew before the next sorrow would overwhelm him and she would hold tighter, willing it to stop.

Eventually it subsided and he pushed away from her, his hand slipping from his eyes to his mouth. Slowly he raised his reddened eyes to her face, seeing her own distress before setting his vision on her shoulder.

'Tell me. Please.' She reached a hand to him, withdrawing it quickly as he flinched at her touch. He tipped his head back against the wall, contemplating the ceiling, his hand dropping to his lap where it lay upturned and immobile like a dead animal adrift on a sea of dark wool.

'You've got to tell me.'

94

'No.' His eyes closed and she turned away, sitting over the edge of the bed with her back to him, feeling the pain in her knees as the blood returned. Her head was cast forward, her hair hiding her face, and she in turn wrapped her arms around herself for warmth and comfort. In a little while he reached a hand to her shoulder and it was her turn to flinch.

'I'm sorry. It was your playing.' His laugh was like a cry as he realised what he had said.

'It wasn't that bad!' She swung at him but he caught her hand, her own tears welling as the relief rose within her.

'No, it was beautiful.' He drew her in and enclosed her with his arms, strong again and dependable. He pulled the covers up around them for warmth as he felt the goose bumps on her slender shoulders, caring once more.

They sat for a long while together, and he watched over her head, the light failing in the sky, the far end of the room descending into shadow. He sighed, smoothing her hair, which raised her eyes and the suggestion of a smile. He knew he should give her some word of explanation, he knew that was what was expected – the right thing to do.

'Just things I haven't thought about for a long time.'

They ate a last meal together, holding hands across the table as if aware more acutely of their parting.

'Tell me, the girl who follows my husband around . . .'

'Magda.'

'Yes, that was it. She's not quite right, is she?'

'Magda is Magda. She sees the world a bit differently, yes. Were you talking with her?'

'Not since the first time here. No, it seemed obvious. It's something in the way she holds herself.' She thought of saying more but decided against, wondering if Michael had worked it out. 'It's lovely. But you always seem to season food with strange emotion.'

'No bitterness, though, gentle one.'

* * *

Her heart flipped at this form of address and for a while she felt like a teenager again, repeating it in her head, with the warmth and richness of the voice which said it, so often that she could not imagine him not saying it again and developing the theme. She was packing the car, coming in and out of the house with bags, humming a tune to herself. Michael emerged, lingering in the doorway, neither inside nor out, looking displeased and getting in the way.

'You seem very pleased with yourself.'

'I'm glad to be getting away.'

'I'd quite like to come with you.'

'Nonsense.' She placed the box she was carrying down on the boot sill, balancing it with her knee. 'You'll have your trees and your "shadow", plenty of nice wine without me around to make you feel guilty. You'll be fine. Besides, they'll be back soon and you'll be too busy to miss me.'

'I didn't mean it like that.' His tone was such that Lucia was actually interested.

'Really? What did you mean?'

'It doesn't matter. My work is good, isn't it? Saleable.' He was the boy again, needing her approval, the approval she was no longer sure she could be bothered to give. Then, when she didn't respond, 'Anyway, hasn't anyone told you?'

'Evidently not.' She was terse in return, irritated by his persistence.

'They're not coming back for ages. They're looking at wolves in Poland. Fuck knows why.'

'Wolves?' she repeated, stupidly.

'Yes. Wolves. Not Little Red Riding Hood wolves. Real ones.'

'Well, they wouldn't be bloody plastic,' she managed under her breath, before slamming the boot lid down, more

96

for effect than anything as she had more to pack, and barging back past him into the house.

Sensing he had gone too far, he offered to help, following her through.

'Where did the guitar come from?'

'Oh, one of the staff gave it to me.'

'You haven't played for years.'

'Well, I thought I might start again. Anyway, I'm taking it to get it valued.'

'It won't be worth much, will it? It's a bit old.'

'It is old and I suspect it might, for a guitar.'

10

Lucia left. He had not realised the extent to which he had come to want her around. Evenings became difficult, dead hours through which he could not settle. He wandered from room to room, simply for the change of scene, lifting a book and flicking at it before laying it aside and moving on. His spirit had forgotten what it was to have time of its own, had forgotten how to avoid the leaden minutes when memories rose to the surface, and with them, old questions. So much had been taken by her now. He drank without pleasure, embracing the indistinction like a lover in whose arms he could lose himself. He knew it would not do; he would wake in the early morning, parched and disorientated, and lie until five or six, trying to lure elusive sleep to come and overwhelm him, extinguishing the guttering flame of his mind, without success. Then, when the time approached for rising, his head would fill with tiredness and his body relax, his joints opening out, so that he would get up ill tempered and unfocused on work.

It was three days before he regrouped. The dogs were grateful, as he exhausted his surplus energy walking them around, taking comfort in the movement of himself and the world around him. The air was thick with birds, flitting between trees or springing up from long grass with an alarm call. The evening light was water to a thirsty man and he drank deeply of it. The trees were in full flush, the beech darkening now and the oak a true green at last. In the meadows lady's smock and *Caltha palustris* were starting in the wetter places, sheens of palest violet intensified by the gentle light, the golden crowns refined.

The exotics of the garden had their beauty but it was a fragile thing. They required care and tending, gentle words and soft handling to solicit their favours. Beautiful and fantastic but enervating. These flowers of the meadow had a subtle beauty. Individually simple and negligible unless inspected closely, but scattered in their thousands and their tens of thousands, adrift on the sea of grass, then they attained greatness. It was a sustaining beauty, feeding the soul, the comforting hand of a friend who makes no demands and expects no response.

He would return before dusk, setting his dew-dampened boots on the kitchen floor by the range to dry, leaving a rime by morning. He would towel off the dogs' bellies, Sally standing square and compliant, lifting each hind leg out and backwards as he worked down it, Phlebus skittish and playful, trying to take hold of the towel for a tussle, shaking it as he would a rat to break its neck. It was a ritual he enjoyed and a routine he was pleased to have returned to. When they had settled before the fire to cook themselves slowly, asleep almost instantly, twitching paws as they pursued the dream of rabbits, he would find himself a bottle and take down a tumbler, reassuringly heavy, and climb up on to the sill of a western facing window. Sometimes he wondered why he bothered with the glass but as he settled himself and cradled it in his lap, he knew the answer. He would sit watching swallows wheeling for late flies and early moths lured by the heat from the walls and the scent of the *Matthiola* he had planted among his herbs. The bats would emerge later and for a while the birds and mammals would fly together, so differently. The birds were masters of speed and grace, the bats like parvenus. They would never collide, though, despite the jittered style, and when the darkness coalesced, the air was left to them. He watched them for as long as he was able until, at last, his eyes failed too and he was left on his perch listening to their clicks and squeaks. Other times, he would pay little attention until dark, content to twirl the amber liquid in his glass, watching the light shattering from the cut surfaces and colouring the wall at his feet.

Somewhere, on the edge of the woods, the bark of a vixen calling cubs, like the sound of a woman being strangled, and the owls, hunting. So many creatures claimed the night and he was glad of it. It was nearly ten when the mild night claimed him too. He closed the door behind himself but stood on the step whilst his eyes adjusted to the moonlight, three-quarters full and crystalline. He rolled himself a cigarette, noting his rapidly diminishing tobacco – another consequence of Lucia's absence – and turned up his collar, more from habit than need.

He had no plan and followed his feet. After several smokes and several stops, they led at last to the Lady's Garden. He put his hand to the well-worn brass handle with sadness. The wisteria was in flower, curtaining the walls with fragrant purple trusses. The darker irises carpeted beneath them with, here and there, lilies – a heady blend of colour and scent, intoxication in the late afternoon. It was at its best for a fortnight at most; a fortnight which condensed a year's labour into splendour. This year it was flowering to no purpose. Lady Palmer was not yet returned, even though it was one of her favourite times, and Lucia was departed. He slipped off his shoes and stepped over the threshold, the ground cold beneath his feet. The blossom hung in pale luminescence, a thousand dimmed lanterns against the darker foliage and he breathed it in before venturing further. He did not get far, a step or two at most, when he became aware of other presences in the night. He peered past the trailing stems and saw. In the middle of the small lawn a pair of male legs, the toes towards him, emerging from under the pneumatic buttocks, light in the darkness, of one of the estate girls. Her back was slender and pleasingly curved above her narrow waist. He could not tell if her hair were black or brown, nor who she was, but her vigour was to be commended. He suspected

Suzie; the style and proportion were right. He observed it in an instant before retreating, closing the door behind him noiselessly, satisfied that the garden was being enjoyed and no longer mournful that it was not by himself. The owner of the legs was the lucky man tonight.

He reacquainted himself with his shoes and, smiling, walked away. His wandering feet took him to the maze, where a conscious purpose resolved within him. He moved through it quickly, knowing the turns and the number of paces required without the need for a greater light. He settled himself upon the table and watched the movement of the stars until long after moonset, the cold working deep within him until later, when he was home again, he would shiver uncontrollably, his jaw clamping hard. For now the sky was bright and he did not think to count the shooting stars which flared and were gone, some blazing colours, or the steady flow of satellites, constant in their speed and direction.

The words broke into his mind like magic, and he remembered his purpose.

'I must take back a trophy to prove I have been here!' he shouted to himself and the rocks around him. Before the final words were formed, the desire was fulfilled and he found himself wrapped in a magnificent, flowing cloak of silver iridescence. Not stopping to admire himself for long, he jumped through the arch and swam up until he thought his lungs would burst with the effort.

When he reached the surface it was morning, so he turned into the golden path of the rising sun and struck out for home. Filled with the joy of living again, he dived out of the water and back under, flashing his cloak in the sunlight, twisting and turning with the pleasure of the surging water over his limbs. Porpoises laughed with him as he swam, and sang a song of boisterous humour to speed him on his way. It was evening when he reached the shore and he could see the lights being lit, up in the houses of the village. He waved his new friends farewell and turned up the track for home. The track itself seemed narrower and the woods closer in than he remembered, but his heart was light and the walking easy as his thoughts turned to Medh. The doors of the houses were shut and bolted when he reached the village as if some fear had come upon the place. He knocked and timid voices were heard from within. He moved from house to house but met with the same invitation, to go on his way, through each door. Puzzled to be turned away by his family, he continued up to the hall where Medh lived. The door was not yet bolted and their night-man let him in. He settled down at the fire with the dogs, who beat the floor with their tails and licked his face in welcome. There he slept the sleep of heroes as if he had not slept in five years.

In the morning Medh found him, stretched out under what appeared to be a pool of shimmering moonlight, his cloak spread around him in the night, covering dogs and floor alike. She gasped when she realised and in the first shame of her nakedness, ran from the hall and out through the fields into the woods. The gasp woke Somhairle, who saw her as the door swung to. He rose and pursued her, the cloak streaming out behind him, as if he were running faster than the wind itself, calling to her all the while, 'Medh! Medh! My heart your prize!'

Medh collapsed by a cool stream in the woods and keened over it, her tears flowing as freely as the waters until they rose and lapped against her knees. Her hair hung about her face like a darkened cloud, her spine a ridge of hills down her slender back. He approached gently, perturbed by the sound and the soft rocking of her body. As he neared, the sores became apparent and the words of the animals returned to him. Felled, as if by an axe, he was on his knees beside her, seeking the line of her face in the troubled waters; his love for her overwhelming him with silence. Unclasping the jewelled pin at his shoulder, he took off the cloak and spread it over her shoulders, not knowing that no cloth had touched her skin for five long years. It was cool against her and peace flowed into her with each breath until the well of her tears ran dry, the stream returning to its natural bounds. Half a day passed before they spoke and in time it was of little things. Half a day more and the voices which had called and called for her fell silent as the light failed in the sky. And still they sat, each looking at the face of the other from the surface of that pool in the woodland stream.

As darkness fell, Somhairle spoke again.

'Come.' And he held out his hand for her.

Together they followed the stream's course down on to the shore and out on to the beach. There the beasts of the woods were waiting, looking out to the ocean as they did each night in restless vigil. Hearing steps on the shingle, they turned.

'Have you brought us our skins, Somhairle?'

'I have lost your skins to the ocean, my friends.'

'Then the curse must stand. You yourself shall feel it.'

'Wait!' Medh stepped forward. 'Wait. Take this cloak of the sea and make new skins. If not a thread is wasted there is just enough for you all.'

The animals saw the wisdom in this and Medh set about cutting and shaping a skin for each. The rising sun saw the task finished and the beasts stood resplendent, catching the new-born light on their flanks. They bowed each in turn and walked back to the stream. There, as the last foot of every animal entered the water, a miracle occurred. Their shapes shifted until they formed mighty fish, strong and sleek with skins of silver iridescence, so brilliant that the water itself shone out. They turned and swam out strongly for the ocean, following the path of the rising sun, the light catching on their fins and sides like a thousand jewels.

He threw himself into his work by day and gradually the standard of the garden revived. It was not that the lads had let it slip exactly, and most would have been more than satisfied with the displays which were developing in the borders, but he felt it was out of focus. It lacked the distinction which his closer involvement brought to it. Michael's excursions had left the immediate vicinity of the Hall clear and the mowing regime was marshalling the grass into proper order, the edges trimmed and as precise as they should be. The gravel paths were raked regularly again and a discipline imposed. Word had been sent and a return date was known at last, a deadline to work to. They could be very exacting when they returned, especially in the first few weeks when their anticipation and the reality collided. The reality needed to be fabulous. He was keeping an eye upon the yew of the maze. The mild season had brought forth a profusion of growth, blurring the lines and narrowing the paths. He would leave it as long as he was able, judging the moment so that any indiscretions would have a chance to recover before being inspected, so that the rest of the garden would not suffer for being left to its own devices.

The lads were in good heart and he was grateful for them. They knew their jobs and did them well and had kept the work going. Four days out of seven were dry and warm, the power of the sun transforming the mood of everyone. They worked into the early evening and ate at the Hall, extending the day willingly, returning the credit of the shorter days of the winter past and the shorter days to come when Lord and Lady Palmer would want times of peace. So it was they were sat around the table, taking time over a glass of beer whilst their dinners settled. There was an hour's tying in to do to end the day. He was drifting in and out of the conversation as his own thoughts possessed him. Ben was teasing Adam about his ragged appearance.

'You're starting to look like him,' indicating their boss sat opposite. Adam laughed, an open, pure sound of a man happy in his world.

'Well, she won't let me rest. She can't get enough.' He gestured rudely.

'Perhaps you don't have enough to give,' Ben retorted. 'Send her to me.'

'You don't have the stamina. The other night . . .'

'Steady, Adam. Pleasures taken in secret gardens should remain secret. I don't think ladies forgive their betrayal.' With that he stood and the others hastened to drain their glasses.

'Rest easy, I've something to attend to first.'

When he was gone, they sat in a disbelieving silence.

'Did he just give you advice?' Ben asked at last.

'I believe he did.'

'Well, there's a first.'

'The iceman thaweth . . . What was that about secret gardens?' Jim asked.

Adam blushed, managing to look horrified, embarrassed and proud in one.

* * *

Michael had uncorked a bottle of Pouilly before the car was out of sight, and stood, watching the dust plumes rising from the wheels as it made its way down the gravelled drive. His trees and his shadow indeed. She always had to know more than him, even when he was trying to surprise her. He resigned himself to not doing anything useful and mooched around the house, unsure of the emptiness. She had taken a number of her pictures with her, something about having them enlarged and printed on linen, she had said, but she had not mentioned which ones. She had been very guarded about her enterprise and selective, he felt, in the pictures he had been shown. She was up to something, as the lie about developing confirmed, and he rootled through her things, looking out the pictures and negatives which remained. In a fold of paper he found a series of different male torsos, lean and muscled, and he found himself standing straighter and trying to pull in his stomach, his free hand descending and cupping his belly protectively. They were static in their execution, each torso off-centre, arms at varying outstretched angles but cut off above the elbow like classically abbreviated statues. Likewise, there were differing lengths of neck showing, from none at all up to an entire Adam's apple, but never faces. It was clear the subjects – or 'objects' as Lucia always insisted somewhat tediously – had not had on a stitch of clothing. The

105

tapering line of the pelvis and muscle at each side of the pictures' bases was pornographic in its suggestion, and the desire which she always denied was evident to even the most myopic. He wondered which of these had given her the 'old and valuable' guitar and just what exactly she had bargained for it. He was fairly sure he knew, but had not expected her to be quite so brazen about leaving the evidence around. He put them away, not caring to restore them to whatever order they had been in. He could see other photographs wrapped in paper and for a minute or two he hesitated, gulping his wine before bracing himself and lifting a second series. At first he could not make out what they were, so abstract were they; angles of light and darkness, apparently random patterns. His eyes grew accustomed to them and he realised the dark areas had texture like hedges. He knew they must record somewhere on the estate but he could not place having seen anywhere like it. Perhaps here was where she had been, those times when he could not find her. He sat thinking and drinking until he fell asleep in the chair.

He slept late, having woken in the night, stiff-necked and cold, and stumbled into bed. He felt lighter in his heart, although his temples seemed to have been clamped in a vice which was tightened and released thirty times a minute. He had wanted to work down by the lake for the next week or so and had requested lunches to be prepared for him, so that he did not have to trudge back, risking his equipment with the vagaries of the weather. He called by the undercroft on his way and found a parcel of food and an empty flask which he filled with coffee from the machine. He searched for the cook to proffer his thanks but the place was deserted. He left a note instead, not wishing to waste any more time.

Magda fell in with him as he left the garden and he was pleased for her company. Her spirits seemed high – as they always did when she seemed there at all – and she laughed at the slightest thing. A tiny blue butterfly, the colour of forget-me-not, crossed their path and she ran after it, arms outstretched, vainly trying to entice it to the flower she had stolen from the border and held up for it now. She tumbled on a hummock, disappearing into the grass, the butterfly settling unconcernedly on a stem near to where she had fallen. Alarmed, Michael set down his things and stepped off the path only to hear laughter ring out from the ground. He laughed too at the joy she found in living, expressed in that sound, but felt sadness for her now like never before. He beamed at her, though, as she poked her head up above the grass with eyes wide, holding her bruised daisy up as if to protect it, though much too late as some of the petals were crumpled and one was torn and lost, breaking the circle. She returned subdued, her face downcast to the flower, her dress creased and stained green at the knees.

'Oh dear, look at you!' Michael tried to modulate his voice like the gardener's.

'Not me, no. I've hurt it.' She held the flower for him to see.

He took it from her and a shadow of alarm puckered her brows until he smoothed back her thick hair, smiling, and placed it behind her ear.

'There. The pretty flower will be safe now.'

She raised a hand and touched at it gently with the tips of her fingers, as if unsure of where the petals began. Feeling it there, she smiled once more. In a few moments it was forgotten and she was skipping along, sometimes behind him, sometimes ahead, singing or humming or stopping to point at something he should see. Haltingly they made their way and haltingly they talked. It was not a conversation as such, she did not seem to feel the need to respond to what he said in any order, but respond she did at some point during the day and usually with much insight. He always wanted to say more than he did, though, and to ask her about herself.

They found a gently sloping strand at the edge of the lough, a mixture of coarse sand and rough pebbles in a slight hollow. From the direction they came it was screened by dense gorse through which they picked a path, following generations of sheep before them whose passing was marked by tears of wool. The sulphur flowers had a scent of coconut and Michael stopped for a minute, looking at the apparent tangle of branches, considering this humble shrub with new eyes. The ovoid spots of harsh colour, soft-edged, the spiny needles glaucous. It was an invigorating inversion which warranted further attention. He nodded to himself as Magda returned, tugging at his sleeve to encourage him on. The low promontory before them held his subject for the week.

'Alder,' he announced to Magda. 'Or at least I think it is.' He felt in his pocket for the *Guide to Trees* he had collected from the library. 'Yes, here it is. Look, *Alnus glutinosa*.' Magda looked, first at the book then at the stand of trees, nodding in recognition before turning away and beginning a search for pebbles of pleasing shape.

'Oval leaves,' he said and, leaving his things, went closer. 'They look round to me. Male catkins, too late for those, and ovoid fruits.' He found what must have been the fruit and turned it over in his hands. It was, in profile, like an egg but the surface was fissured to the core all over and it looked more like a skeleton of what had been. He could not imagine it bearing life. Fortunately, that was not what he had come for and he crouched down to where the roots twisted and arched over the edge of the bank. Some had been undercut so that a space lay behind, the roots forming a cage. He looked underneath and could see a clear soil profile, a veneer of peaty black above a deep layer of silver sand. He slipped off his shoes and socks and rolled his trousers up, bracing himself as he paddled into the cold waters of the lough. Further round, some trees reached down into the very water and as the waves lapped with a gurgle-slap he watched them appear and disappear. He thought perhaps he could paint one in water, one whose roots grasped the air, and another which had germinated all those years ago atop a large rock, the roots now enclosing it like a fist as they reached for the soil beneath. Three approaches to living in this hostile place where little else seemed to manage except for the gorse and some scrubby grass, more brown than green. He looked a while longer, then, as it was nearly time, thought lunch could be in order.

Magda fell upon the food like a hungry bird. It was clear she had given no thought to it. There was more than enough food for one but slightly short for two and he divided it as best he could, trying to reserve for himself the larger share. She did not appear to mind and he guessed from her build that she did not eat that much anyway. There were the inevitable sandwiches but the soft cheese was good and he did not think he could ever tire of the bread. A slice of meat pie proved harder to divide, the short pastry crumbling as he attempted it. Magda waved a hand at him, bouncing slightly on her haunches and looking annoyed.

'No.' She leaned forwards and bit a piece off as he held it, her hand on his to steady it. The crumbs coated her lips and glistened there until she swallowed before a sweep of her tongue cleared them away. He swallowed too.

'Good pie?'

She nodded and the division continued amicably until the chicken leg. Michael adored chicken and the chicken here had been a revelation, moist and flavoured like no chicken he had tasted before. He had even asked what they had fed them on and thought they were laughing at him when they told him. He wasn't to know, was he? They each reached for the chicken at the same time and for a moment were like dogs with a bone, exerting a pull. He gave way first and Magda bit greedily, watching him. He could not help himself looking sad and after she had swallowed she held it out for him but would not relinquish it. Bite by alternate bite the leg was consumed, the flesh picked clean until only the bone remained, clutched in Magda's fist.

After lunch he set up his equipment and Magda, as was her habit, positioned a box slightly behind and to the side of him so that she could see the canvas and the subject without moving. Sometimes she sang, sometimes she hummed, but he noticed after a while that her tune had fallen in time with the wash of the waves as the slight breeze licked the surface of the waters. It was not cold in the sun but the air, cooled as it was from its passage, held little residual heat, and he found himself warming and cooling as the cloud passed.

He was working hard and trying to concentrate, although his mind kept returning to Lucia's pictures, knowing how close she must have been to take them. He had painted nudes and Lucia had never seemed concerned – it was natural after all. He had slept with some of them too – but really, how could he not when it was expected? That his wife might have the same desire did not seem appropriate, he had thought of her as somehow purer than that. Besides, she showed little interest in sex, except occasionally. His carryings-on had been sordid and he knew it, but to think she knew it too . . . He kicked himself for not bringing the abstracts. Magda could perhaps have told him where it was.

'Now then. What do you think so far?' He leaned back from the half-finished picture but did not turn until, there being no response, he glanced behind.

Magda was wading out into the water, feeling her way with her toes over the uneven rocky floor, the surface so disrupted with the waves that sight was useless. The water was lapping over her knees and her arms were outstretched for balance, just as they had been that first time he had seen her. He was stunned by her naked beauty, staring open-mouthed, his brush forgotten and drooping in his hand, dripping paint on to the ground where it fizzled and sank into the dry sand. She had stopped, undecided about what to do next, the water at the top of her thighs, each wave rising up against her, making her shriek. As if aware she was being watched, she started to turn, Michael hurriedly lowering his gaze. Unbalanced, she splashed backwards, twisting as she did so, affording him a further treat. He ran forward, brush in hand, but she was there, head above the surface, laughing and waving before turning on her front and swimming out towards the low island, her hair flowing out behind her like black snakes.

He was shaking and he laid aside his brush, scooping up the cold water and splashing his face with it, blinking hard.

11

The week continued much as it had begun. Michael requested more food and explained why, receiving an ambivalent smile in return which left him feeling uncertain. Magda was beyond surety and doubt. Like an animal she moved through the world, lithe and loose-limbed, taken first by one curiosity then another, investigating what others would consider mundane with the same intensity as she had for what others would consider worthy of note. On the second day, when he had intended to paint quickly, just in case, he had become entranced by Magda's pebble cataloguing on the strand. Pretending to be thinking about what came next in his composition, he watched her from the corner of his eye, just as he would with a blackbird so as not to scare it. Like a bird she picked her way barefoot over the stones, stopping now and then, turning her head one way then the other before diving down and scooping up a pebble almost as if it might escape were she any slower. Whenever she had collected five in this way she returned to her 'nest' – a small circle of sand she had painstakingly cleared of stones and the twiggy jetsam which lay about. Here she considered each one, weighing it in her hands, turning it in the sunlight, firstly dry and then with a wetted thumb applying a smear of saliva to clean and darken it. She squeezed each one in her fists as if to feel their true solidity, to get as close to them as she could. He watched entranced, unable not to stare, as she laid a stone in the palm of her left hand and ran the tip of her forefinger over it, firstly with her eyes open, correlating the surface and the feeling then, magically, his heart quickening, she closed her eyes slowly, deliberately, her lips parting as she repeated the exercise blind, a small smile forming as the connection with the memory was made. After she had done this with all her stones she began to place them with great care. A second time she lifted each in turn and stared at it as if to see its very nature, before deciding where it should go. He was baffled by the pattern which began to emerge, the larger and the smaller, the lighter and the darker stones did not seem to conform to any alternation or grouping he could discern. The circles formed gradually from arcs but only as she finished could he see that they were interlinked, one larger than the other. Magda seemed pleased with her work, not the easy pleasure she took from the world around her but a quieter, fuller satisfaction. She rocked back on her heels, nodding slightly and he could see her eyes were tracing the circles. When she was done she looked over to him. He set down his brush and went over, crouching beside her, risking a hand on her shoulder as he did so. She did not flinch. At first he did not realise what he was seeing and his confusion drew him in. He knew she had started with sixteen stones, as he had watched her intently whilst she hunted; three times five had she stooped before hoarding, then once more, one crucial last time which took as long to select a single stone as all the others. Now he counted nine stones in each circle. He stopped and counted again, starting in a different place, though their random forms seemed to make it harder, if anything, and he glanced around the circumferences comparing likenesses. There were nine in each and sixteen in total – he had not been wrong. It was beautiful and unexpected and he took up her hand and squeezed it, holding her attention.

'Good, Magda. It's very good.'

She curtained her face with her hair and extricated her hand and he felt he might have missed the point. He looked at the rings on his own for a while before returning to his easel. He could not see what other reaction she could have wanted and felt hurt at the rejection.

He painted solidly until lunch, trying to forget the annoyance he felt at his inability to read her. He was working on the alder which grasped the air. He had mixed dark tones for the twisting roots and the grass above so that the void behind the roots would be tonally the same but less intense, an absence of black rather than the presence of white. He was introducing light from the front although he knew it would be considered wrong to do so. It felt right, though, just as the choice of subjects always felt right. He was amazed really, both by the world and himself. Trees had always been wallpaper, a backdrop hardly worthy of notice. Now, as he thought, he realised he had never seen an unattractive tree and certainly not an ugly tree. There had been mutilated trees with torn or twisted branches, withered stumps snapped off above their supports, though what effort must have been required on the part of the idle youths to achieve these things he could only imagine. Old people or unattended pets were surely softer and more gratifying targets. The pollarding seemed fairly brutal too. The tree surgeons swinging about on ropes forty or fifty feet aloft, curing the trees of growth, amputating the boughs, delimbing with a buzz of high-pitched annoyance. Ground workers would collect the waste, feeding it into a mulcher which droned away, spewing out a stream of pale chips into a skip. He had sat in the pub on the corner watching them work whilst Lucia shopped and he supposedly visited the museum. It had taken so little time, a pint or a pint and a half at most, to abbreviate a tree. With barely a pause the surgeons were down on the ground for a word or two of chat, their visors raised, their ear muffs pitched up on to their helmets like compound eyes – then they were high again in a blur of saws, a twisted aerial ballet of syncopated rhythms. Like army ants, there was a collective purpose to their work, although little seemed to be said once they were in the sky. It was a few months before he was back that way and the trees were double rows of lollipops, lush ovoids contained and proscribed, nothing really but a condiment, a garnish to the street.

Magda was not so much sullen as elsewhere throughout lunch, toying with a sandwich but setting it aside half-eaten. He tried to tempt her with some chicken but she waved it away and the fruit cake held a similar lack of interest. He found himself chewing joylessly, oppressed by her attitude and the lack of communion between them. It was clear she did not want to eat, but nor did it seem she wished to do anything else. She sat there, for a while poking at the food, for a while looking at him but apparently bored and restless. His attempts to engage her in conversation went the same way as the chicken, it was as if he did not matter and he started to feel as much. He gave up and fell instead to wondering why she stayed, unless it was so that he could see her suffer, if that was what she was doing.

He lay back, propping himself on an elbow and looking out at the water, almost at eye level, watching the light play on the wave crests. There were many things in his life about which he was not happy. He had never really had a clue about life generally or what to do. Some of his peers had forsaken art for advertising and were doing very well, or so it seemed. No point wasting too much time on what-might–have-beens and he occupied himself with a cigarette, trying to remember how many cartons were left back at the house. That was one thing about living all this way from anywhere – they had to be organised. Many of them appeared to smoke and there was no evidence of the fields of tobacco which would be required to supply them all. He could not imagine the plants thriving here in the wet, anyway, though he did not understand why he might be having that thought.

He forsook the convolutions of his thought for something he had not done since he was young, too young in fact to do it well. He started to search for pebbles, methodically turning this way and that, stopping to lift one before discarding it if its underlying form, not apparent from above, was unsuitable. Magda seemed intrigued but was still playing the mystic, so he left her to it. He filled the ample pockets of his trousers so that the pleats of them bulged, making him look fatter. He weighed the last stone in his hand and turned his left shoulder to the water, bending slightly from the waist, leaning backwards. He unleashed a stone with a flick of the hand, a large, fine-grained disc which hit the water with a slap then skip, skip, skipping on before breaking the surface and disappearing. Only a four, though the distance was good. Magda was engaged again and ran over, standing too close to him so that he could not throw until he had taken a step away. He plunged a hand into his pocket and selected a small rock which he hoped he could skim more. He lowered himself further to reduce the angle, watching the licks of spume erupt on the water as the stone skittered out, finally running over the surface barely lifting, in too many hits to count.

'Again!' Magda shrieked, bouncing and clapping.

He took a larger stone and threw for fewer bounces and less distance, sacrificing them both for height, risking the angle with great force but heaving the stone back from the water once, twice, before it splashed with a loud gurgle. He was lost in the pursuit and even Magda's excitement came to him as if from a long way off, from the future in which he would find himself when he stopped, when the last stone sank beneath the waves, where life had become complicated and full of effort. Until then he was a child in a world of intuition, the compromise between the shape and the weight, the natural, unconscious force required to get the best result, the surprise and adjustment required when it did not work out as expected.

When he was done he sighed, standing square with both hands immersed in his pockets. The work was pressing on his mind and he knew he would be glad when this time was over. The isolation these people had chosen was not to his liking. The goings-on were too involved, the relationships too personal. It exerted a pull on him, no doubt, just as the water inevitably pulled a stone into itself, the liquid parting and reforming, the stone disappearing from sight. He could see that such a closeness would have benefits, the closeness of being cared for and accepted. But to be known in that way, known daily and have all that expectation of how you are as a person and why you do the things you do. No. Deeply troubling and not for him, not now and hopefully not ever. What sense of freedom could they have, shut in by these hills and all that knowledge? The small glass bottle which awaited him in the refectory the day before had confirmed all his fears; the note from 'that man', as he had come to think of him: 'If you are working by the water, this might help against the midges.' He stretched at his collar, even though it was not tight, to ease the claustrophobia. Magda was tugging at his sleeve and holding up a stone for him. It was a perfect skimmer, even of weight and form, flattened appropriately, the right size to hand.

'You try.'

She turned without a word and adopted the stance, and he thought for a moment that she might be mocking him in the way she positioned herself. She glanced at him, biting at her lower lip, seemingly at a loss for words, just as she had been all day. The stone cut into an oncoming wave, the leading edge too sharp. For no reason he could fathom, it filled him with sadness and he twisted his face in his attempts to smile for her. He took time to teach her, patiently explaining the ideas of angles and force and bidding her watch his movements and copy them, hoping that by one way or another she would learn. The first stone she managed thrilled her and another wave of remembrance swept over him, but his words were genuine and kind and she collected more. For a time they played together, competing stone by stone, though he was pulling his throws to encourage her.

Eventually he could avoid his work no longer and he left her there at the water's edge. He lifted the brown bottle from his kit bag and dabbed oil at the back of his neck and round his ears before lighting one more cigarette. Magda preyed on his mind. The next time he looked around her dress lay over a rock like the sloughed skin of a snake, diaphanous, the cloth lifting in the breeze as if agitated. He looked to the sky as the temperature dropped, amazed that only a thin, wispy cloud was obscuring the sun and would soon be passed. She was reaching the island, which seemed to hold some sort of fascination for her, and he watched as she pulled her pale body from the dark waters, her black hair streaming down the middle of her back. She was too far away for him to see clearly and his surreptitious desire sat within, uncomfortable and unfulfilled. He set down his brush and palette, taking a cloth from the top of one of his boxes and wiping his hands methodically, pulling each finger through a fold of the fabric and working around the nails until all traces of colour were gone. He stroked her dress, his fingers running down the shoulder and round the scoop of the neck, feeling the simple cotton between his thumb and forefingers. He replaced it just as it had been, smoothing out the creases with a flat hand, not noticing the smudge of sienna he left on the hem. Magda was sat on a rock which looked as if it overhung the water. Her legs were pale roots spread over the stone in their search for water, her feet finding it. He could see from the splashes that she was kicking through the larger waves as they lapped below her.

* * *

He had collected some food to take back to the house to eat alone, his pack set down in the hall where it could rest untroubled by the attentions of Lucia. He could not find a clean glass and slopped wine into a tumbler, wiping a line of grease from the rim before draining a good half of it. He collected a couple of pictures with which he had not been entirely happy and set them against the wall across from the table so that he could look at them whilst he ate. It took times of patient looking and the remembering of what had been seen to judge the quality of what he had done. The food was not helping him concentrate and he pushed it aside, taking up his cigarettes in its place. The more he looked the less satisfied he became, and he drank his way through the first bottle remorselessly. The pictures were good, technically excellent, a degree of innovation – nothing radical or movement-gener- ating, admittedly – a degree of imagination, just the right amount indeed to convey arborality or whatever the adjective might be, whilst deepening the understanding of the viewer. He lurched upwards, knocking the now empty glass over on to the table where it described arcs before settling, and set off for cigarettes and a review of all his work since arriving.

Savagely he removed the oaks from the passageway and carried them through. He collected the others and brought them, together with more wine. He started well, giving time to each one, looking critically at the technical merits or other- wise. As the evening advanced and he drank more, the time spent looking and the time spent whirling between them evened out; he was drawing heavily all the while, although he knew he had only two packets left after this one, turning, his face twisted and his lips tight across his teeth in a rictus of disgust. He sank into a chair, embedding his cigarette-laden hand into his hair dangerously. The smoke caught in a draught from the open door and drifted down over his left eye in a spiral. There was no birdsong; there was no fucking birdsong.

He was back at his Finals Exhibition, the people milling, look- ing at each other as much as the art, gossiping. Lucia was late. She had always been late, it seemed, running in flushed, dis- rupting the speeches with a clever remark, or waltzing in in splendour, deliberately overdressed in wine-dark silk, a choker of black pearls at her throat, shaming them all in their rags, disrupting the speeches with her silent challenge. She had grown out of the latter at least. He was checking his watch and fiddling with his collar, alone and largely unknown, his friends not yet arrived, not appreciating just how important this was to him. A couple of hacks had a look of profound boredom as they passed him and he sneered down his nose at their backs.

'Nothing exceptional.'

'Pleasant.'

Their laughter took them beyond his hearing. The show had been well received and there had been some sales and a wider expression of future interest. He was haunted by nothing exceptional and every time he received praise the suspicion of insincerity would eat at him, the thought that he was just being indulged, humoured like a child.

He bit round his thumbnail, tasting some paint which he had failed to shift earlier. There was not much left to chew and he turned his attention to the other one, working at it until the skin tore down the edge and a spot of blood flowered there. His eyes ached and he pressed at them, though it would not help, and the muscles at the base of his neck were tight but there was no one to loosen them. Memories of Magda burned in his mind. She was becoming a sun in his world. He had begun to see her dresses like thin summer clouds which lessened the heat momentarily, veils of morning mist hanging low in the valley, lingering there until the heat of the afternoon sun burned them away. When he closed his eyes he could see her in the distance, pulling herself out of the water on to the island – a still of memory almost devoid of colour. Or again on the rock, the white clouds forming behind as if to eclipse her, held back by the tall dead trees, twisted and black like the piers of a broken bridge.

He found himself in the studio, picking out the smallest canvas he had. The weave was tight and he ran his eye over it, appraising the texture it would reveal through the paint. Too much was his conclusion and he mixed a wash the colour of the breasts of the small collared doves which would fly up from the grass at the woodland edges and sit in the trees just beyond reach, staring boldly as he walked by as if defying him to fly. He covered it all, leaving a smooth surface with which to begin were he to have need of it. The new possibilities quietened him and he regretted the drinking. He plunged his head under the cold tap in the kitchen until his mind began to clear. As he straightened the water ran down his chest and back in icy rivulets which made him shudder but which seemed necessary somehow. He towelled his hair and drank glass after glass of water, as much as his stomach could cope with, to aid his chances in the morning. He ate a mouthful or two of food, the flavours of which had intensified with the cooling, and gave up on the day.

* * *

The morning began with a drizzling mist which cleared as the cloud lifted into a thoroughly rain-soaked day. Michael sat in the upstairs lounge, his feet in slippers up on the rosewood desk, his legs crossed at the ankles. His sketchpad was on his knee and everything he needed was within reach. He was thinking of Magda's movements and the ways in which she held herself, drawing cartoons of her as he had seen her and as he would like to see her. He thought perhaps he could subvert the classical ideal, having her slip from her dress not as some tame Venus, civilised by consumption and convention, but as a feral creature rejecting her clothes, issuing a challenge. He enjoyed this fantasy through the morning, working on details, working out on the page how she could be captured. From time to time he would rise and wander over to the window and, perching on the sill, smoke in consideration of the world.

By lunchtime he was getting hungry, having finished off the supper from the night before for breakfast. He had become so accustomed to being outside that he craved it, finding the walls lacking in stimulation somehow, used to the . . . birdsong, the changes in the light, the minute fluctuations of temperature which composed a day. He wandered to the Hall, eating lunch alone as always, it seemed, before heading to the library.

The shutters were closed when he entered and he folded them back, the light, such as it was, spilling in, melancholy with the green paint. The settee was covered with a dust sheet, as were the chairs, and a decorative screen was across the fireplace; a silver peacock displaying for somebody to see for the first time in months. He ran his fingers along the edge of the bare desk, the dust lifting, leaving a smear of bright, honeyed wood beneath. It was cool to the touch – beyond cool, cold – and he felt the absence of the owner's life in the room. He sat himself in the buttoned leather chair, his hands grasping the padded arms, his fingers exploring the line of upholstery studs which marked a mineral boundary between plant and animal, rotating one way then the other. He spun slowly round, though he remembered what he would see. The room was entombed in books except for the oriel, which remained free. He wondered what happened to the new acquisitions for the collection which he had seen on this very desk before. Perhaps there was a sub-library or an archive where old books went to die, their places taken by the recent additions, freshly returned from the binders where they had been made to look old.

When he had tired of playing the master he meandered over to the section he had come to view for inspiration, pausing on his way to pour a whiskey which would fell a carthorse. Evening fell almost imperceptibly, so dark had the day become, but with it came an idea of how the picture should be. Magda would be central and to the fore. Behind her would be water stretching out to the left and to the right, divided by the island on which he would paint the five skeleton trees. Their crowns would intermesh forming a screen behind her head – a lattice in silhouette. Her dress would be round her waist or just below, her wrists still caught by the shoulder straps, hunching her shoulders and perplexing her face, downcast. That would all be as nothing when compared to her eyes.

It was the afternoon of the fifth day since Lucia's departure. A postcard had arrived that morning, telling of people seen and good times; her meetings seemed to be taking place in bars. Her laughter ran through it and he missed her as he read it; she had always seemed better from a distance. The sun's heat had been waxing throughout and had beat down on his neck and the back of his head after lunch, making him close and edgy. The breeze had been dropping, stilling the water which stretched away to his side, glassy and inviting. He felt he had been imagining it and he concentrated, barely touching the last of the alders. The birds had stopped singing. There was a gentle wash from the water on the shore but nothing else. No other sounds. He stopped pretending to paint and looked to the sky, breathing in the heat which was lifting from the strand. His head was tight at the temples like a migraine-in-waiting and he rubbed the back of his neck, feeling the skin hot beneath his hand. He sipped at the water bottle, holding the liquid in his mouth until it thickened and cloyed before swallowing. A man's body appeared in his mind without prompting and he shook it away, turning to offer Magda the water.

Magda was at the water's edge, her dress lifted up to her knees as she tested the temperature like every other day. She was magical; so absorbed in the present to the exclusion of all else. She was feeling the bottom tentatively with her toes. He knew what would come next. She returned to the dry ground and slipped from her dress, laying it over the rock she always chose. He did not look away, nor did she. She was easy in herself and unashamed as he stared at her, naked and splendid, barely concealing his desire.

'Swim,' she said.

Hesitantly he began to undress, starting with his shoes and socks, placing each sock in the correct shoe for re-dressing.

He took his trousers off first, she watching impatiently rather than interested. He unbuttoned his shirt, drawing in his stomach as he peeled it from his arms. She had not looked away throughout and he was left feeling ashamed of the turgor in his shorts, willing it to subside.

He walked towards the water, wincing as its frigidity washed over his feet. Magda strode boldly and his pride bolstered him. The groin threshold was a trial to them both and they laughed together as the gentle swell lapped against them. They shared a smile and a resolution before diving on the count of three, she so gracefully, curving out of the water and back into it like a wave of the lough itself, leaving the surface untroubled.

They swam out together, so close that their hands almost touched as they swept back. Within a few strokes she began to pull ahead and though he exerted himself, puffing and heaving at the water, he fell behind. At water level the island seemed further away and he began to fear the dark waters of the lough swirling beneath him in unknown depths.

When he was over half-way there, Magda pulling herself from the water ahead of him, he heard the first thunder, menacing and low over the hills. He raised his eyes to the mountain, seeing how the cloud had developed there. He kicked out with renewed vigour, the island approaching with each stroke. The rain burst on the surface around him, springing up in splashes and shattering the reflection of the cloud into a thousand million facets. The thunder was louder and from the corner of his eye he thought there was a flash. Magda was waving and hopping and he could see her concern but it was the best he could do. Finally he got there and she grasped his hand to pull him out, almost dropping him again as a loud crack broke in the air above them. They crouched in the lee of a stone wall as the world grew dark around them, the far shore disappearing behind a curtain of rain, the lightning flashes contrasts through the gloom. They huddled together for warmth, his arms around her, feeling the goose bumps on

124

her skin, his teeth chattering uncontrollably as he cooled from the swim and the adrenalin leached from his blood.

An hour or two hours may have passed, it would have made no difference, life was suspended until the storm was over. He tried not to think of the body in his arms, yet inevitably the awareness would come to him and he fought hard to think of other things. He stroked her hair, over and over, with occasional noises of comfort. The ease she had with herself was astonishing; the trust she placed in him. In time the storm moved on beyond the mountain, leaving the sky clouded but still, coloured intermittently by the lightning. They stood and rubbed themselves to get some warmth back.

The water was a steely grey, cold and inviolable. With displeasure they lowered themselves into it, surprised by its residual warmth, warmer than the air. They swam back together, Magda holding her stroke so as not to leave him behind this time. They broke the still waters with their hands, sending out ripples of disruption. The trees behind them reflected black in the grey water and he was glad when they had cleared the last searching fingers of twig and broke into clear water.

12

Dear Anna,

*My sweetest friend. You shouldn't have worried about asking;
of course, it makes sense. Send the papers and I'll sign them.
Patrick is a good man and I've been very glad for you since
you've been together.*

*Life without love is a shadow, a wind which blows first one
way then another, inconstant and tiring. That you are together
makes me easier for you and yes, I can imagine you smiling as
you read this, it lessens my feelings of guilt.*

*Things are much the same here. Magda's continued fascina-
tion with painting has speeded up the work in the gardens and,
according to Elsie, the kitchens too. Did you know that when
birds moult in the summer they stop singing? It is an eerie,
quiet period, at odds with the life of the rest of the season. I feel a
bit the same, not having her around so much. As if life has flown
away for a while. I try to keep an eye on her when I can. Elsie
tells me I am jealous. She could be right.*

Love S x

* * *

He set down his pen, considering the page barely half-filled
with words and the darker drops of ink where his hand had
lingered over letters. He had thought she would have asked
before, years before, and now that it had happened it left him
feeling strange. It had been many years since he had walked
away from that life. He remembered every detail from those
last few hours, which had begun when he set down his pen,
this pen, mid-sentence on his desk, not bothering to clean the

nib or replace the lid. He stood and stretched, cracking his ribs and shoulders, hunched as he had been for so many months over Derrida and Lacan, Unamuno and Hegel. Picking up his wallet from where it sat next to a silver relief of Tam galloping over the bridge, pursued by witches who grabbed at Meg's tail and by flying demons bearing down on him, walking out into the incessant rain without his coat. Walking to the station, being splashed by cars through oil-slicked puddles, miring his cream trousers, only stopping to withdraw cash from the machine he passed on his way.

He caught a train heading west into the banked cloud at the end of the platform. He did not know, then or now, whether he had intended to come here or to stop at Bahir. When he had reached Bristol the decision had been made and he would not see Bahir again. He bustled his way to the telephones which smelt of grease and piss and left a message on the machine as he had hoped, saying he would be away a week or ten days and not to worry. Whilst he had stood for an hour looking out over the rank and the rain, the melancholy taxis collecting the unloved to take them wherever, Anna had returned and hearing those last, uncharacteristic words, had rung the police, shaken, to report him missing. He had not been absent long enough, he was an adult after all and there was nothing they could do. When they started looking, he was gone.

He had thought about it a lot in the early days. The guilt primarily, if that was what it was. The artificial ending, so forced, so willed as if their lives had broken off mid-sentence leaving much remaining to be said. They would call it madness, he knew that, or a breakdown if they were being kind. But, like a suicide, the time for living the expectations of others had passed, and he did not answer the many letters that were sent. There is more than one way a man can die and that life was death to him. In time it had faded, though he found himself obsessing about her at certain times of year, or thoughts of her would arise unprompted and unwanted and he would find them difficult to shake.

She had come out, the one time she had visited, bringing him things he had left behind that she had thought he might want or need: a few clothes, his guitar, the picture of herself in a silver frame looking young and beautiful from their early days together. He could not look at it now without seeing her as he had that last time, her eyes ringed with tiredness and her mouth pinched at the corners. Such a full and beautiful mouth, always smiling or smouldering but never sad before then. Later she had sent a picture of herself and Patrick, sun-bathed on the deck of a boat, the aquamarine sea and ochre land behind suggestive of the hotter Mediterranean. It had not rewritten his memory. She was healed but the scar he had left on her remained. The unframed picture of himself and Max, an odd choice he had thought, but he had kept it all the same. And hard words full of pain, after which they had walked for a long while on the lough shore, holding hands and silence.

The day she left they took a boat out and they rowed to the island, finding peace there. They made love in a hollow of wiry grass behind the ruined chapel wall, watched over by the ravens from their rambling nest, high in the branches of the pine above them. It was a long time ago. Now they were parting for a third time, a third little death, and he considered her letter, wondering if this would be the final end between them. He did not think so, but marriage could change people as he himself knew. He read it through a second and final time before consigning it to the fire of the range just as he had with all the others. It was difficult to avoid the accumulation of matter, the amassing of artefacts which bound a person to the earth, without direct action.

The ink of his letter was dry and he folded the page and sealed it in an envelope. He would drop it by the Hall in the morning and it could go with the general mail. He wetted his tongue with a sip of water, tasting the glue for a second time, and rolled a cigarette, taking it outside and sitting on the step with the dogs for company. Phlebus settled over his feet,

Sally standing at his knee to have her ear caressed. She sneezed as the smoke caught in her nostrils. The evening air was mild and seductive and he begrudged the necessity of having to go to bed to be fit for work. He could hear the distant bluster of the wind through the treetops, brief but insistent, and he sensed a turn in the weather. There were owls hunting but little else, and he felt, not for the first time, that the wider world could have ceased to be.

* * *

The day started dry and warm, lifting the dew, which rose from the ground and flowed up the slopes over the tips of the grass. He had stopped at Sun's Rest to examine the oak. From near the fissured top had sprouted new growth, the coppered leaves late and small and more akin to a sapling rooted in a cleft of a rock face than a renewal by the tree itself. He was amazed, as ever, by the determination of life. As he looked he could see two small black eyes, points of coal-light, from the gnarled bole. He stared and the weasel stared, bobbing once, twice on its hind legs before turning and flowing back into its hole like a sock on a string.

When he reached the bothy he was surprised to find Jack there ahead of him, and they shook hands as they always had. Jack was a reassuringly solid type who always seemed to wear the same clothes, day after day, summer or winter. He lifted his cloth cap and rubbed his hand over his pate, his frown following his hand back in a wave of furrows. He was not one for drama or unnecessary words but he appeared to be building up to something.

'Tea, Jack?'

'Please.' He settled himself at the bench, running his hand over the wood, his eye working professionally, unable to stop himself.

The gardener watched him with half an eye, happy to let him take his time. When he had received his tea and sniffed twice he spoke out.

'Could you come and have a look at an oak for me?'

'Of course, no trouble. I'm sure it won't matter if I'm elsewhere for a day. I'll set the lads on first but we're just ticking over really at the minute.'

'I've asked Simon. He'll be here when he's checked the barns.'

'Simon? A council of war, huh?' Simon was good with his trees, though it was not his training, and a useful worker if heavy work was required.

'Aye. Well. I think I'd like you to see for yourselves. I've not seen anything like it before.'

'Hmm. We'll take a couple of saws then, shall we?'

'It might be for the best.'

Jack's placid face had an anxiety about it which he had not seen before. Unusually, he kept no animals or pets and would joke about it if anybody suggested he might or tried to offer him something, saying he had trouble enough looking after himself without dependants to worry for. He left Jack starting to clean out an already clean pipe of dark cherry wood on briar, one he had made for himself, whilst he went to sort two chainsaws, mixing fuel and oil, enough for a day of cutting if required. It was clear Jack cared for his trees, even in their thousands and their ten thousands.

They rode across the park three abreast with Lucy reined in behind carrying the tools and food. The horses were frisky in the morning sun, happy to be moving together and wishing to run. Early midges bit the men and large black flies rose from the grass and swabbed around the horses' mouths and eyes, making them toss their heads and snort. Some protection was afforded by smoking and Simon cursed them both for the pleasure they were taking in their tobacco. The biting insects could not lessen the beauty of the day, though, and as they rode down by the lough, taking time to water the horses ahead of the climb into the woods, there was pleasure in each others' company. They turned their backs to the Hall and the figures of Michael and Magda meandering down, and cut on to the ride, pausing before they did so to watch the wisps of mist blowing up through the canopy of the woods on the far side until, clearing the tree line, they were dispersed by the winds, vanishing into clear sky.

The woods were vibrant with the late spring growth. The musty earthiness of the leaf litter formed a base over which the rich scent of wild garlic would collect in sheltered places, though now and then as they rode a draught of fresher air carrying the faintest tints of verdancy from the leaves of hazel and birch would refresh them. In dappled shade primroses lingered and dark native bluebells spiked through the grass, glowing from the ground. When they passed out from under the canopy the sun was warm on their backs and the horses would respond with whinnies and tail-flicking. It took nearly the hour to reach the tree and, as Jack said, it was obvious when they had found the one. They dismounted and slackened the girths of the horses before tethering them at the edge of the glade where they could have shade if they desired it and lush grass.

The oak in question stood in a small clearing and had grown straight and evenly. It was a beauty, or had been a beauty, of about eighty years, in the prime of its youth. The bole, whilst not huge, had begun to thicken and the bark was developing its deep fissures which had already been colonised on the northerly aspect by ferns and lichens. The grass thinned in the deeper shade and bugle predominated, sending up its spires of indigo flowers which in bud seemed almost black. The cool humidity refreshed them as much as the water they sipped from the bottles they had brought. Jack caressed the tree, looking to the faces of the others, who had retreated to the edge and were looking up, considering. The leaves had opened and the canopy had been full but now they could see into it as if time had reversed, and there, near the centre, was a jay's nest, the owner flying out and away in a blur of buff and blue, shouting a warning to the world.

'When did you say you were here last, Jack?' Simon shouted across.

'Before yesterday, be three weeks since.'

'And it was fine then?'

'I'm telling you, it was like the others.' And he waved an arm around the glade to the trees which stood guard over them.

They believed him – he was not a man to be mistaken about such a thing – and they considered the other oaks, full in growth and health.

'It's awful quick,' he said, before exhaling smoke in a flurry at the clouds of midges which had found them.

'Are you thinking phytophora?' Simon glanced quickly at him.

'Are you not?'

'I don't know what else it could be. It's not water stress,' he admitted.

'We'll have it down and burnt. I know it's severe but we can spare this one for the sake of the others.' And then to Jack he shouted, 'We'll take her down Jack, I think.'

'That's what I reckoned too.' Shaking his head with regret, not denial.

It took a sparse few minutes for Simon to fell the tree; it had taken longer for them to decide among themselves who had done so most recently. There was not much call for it on the estate and they all felt unpractised, discussing the job with more care than was normal. Sparse minutes in which the saw whined seven times and seven times only, ending the life which had been longer than theirs. He narrowed the bole at the base to start with, cutting downwards obliquely to the bark to make it easier for the final felling cuts. The wedge came out cleanly and he paused, lifting his visor to examine the timber, which revealed nothing out of the ordinary; the cambium was moist and ruddy. There may have been staining, but it was difficult to tell. It would not have been right to abort the operation at that point; he was committed. He hun-

132

kered down and revved the engine, touching the chain to the flesh into which it sank as if without resistance. As it cleared the bark they could hear the change in the engine note as the heartwood, hard and dense, increased the work of the chain. It cracked from the hinge, pausing for a fraction of a moment as if undecided, as the wood made its final stand against gravity then crashed down in a shattering of branches and twigs, breaking and flying through the clearing. He killed the saw and set it aside and they left the horses, which had bridled at the high-pitched noise and destruction, even though they had led them further into the trees. Lucy, typically, was fine, being used by exposure to loud work. His ears were laid back and flattened and his rear hoof poised 'on point' as if he were about to kick, but that was as normal.

Simon was looking relieved in the glade and Jack clapped a hand on his shoulder and nodded, seeing the pulse at his temple.

'A job well done.'

Simon replied with a half-smile, his face pale.

'You'll take up smoking one day, when you see sense.' And he inserted his pipe into the groove which similar pipes, smoked over a lifetime of pipes, had worn into his teeth. Often he held one there whether it was lit or not. 'It helps me to think,' he would say if anyone teased, or, 'I'd sooner do without an arm than my pipe.'

They poked around the fallen crown, finding the jaylings, which had been thrown from their nest, dazed but otherwise unharmed. They had trouble catching the three of them amid the tangle of branches, as they ran and fluttered, squawking all the while. Jack placed them in the crook of a wide branch near to where the adult had flown, cradling each strange creature in his hands, trapping their heads between his work-thickened fingers as they struggled to peck in a vain attempt at escape, hoping their calls would lure the adult back and they would be fed for the week which would see them fledged, before setting off in search of kindling.

Whilst he was gone they began the slow task of dismembering the tree. Fortunately it was a large, broad crown and there was enough room to allow them both to work safely. They cut their way inwards, no fancy work of regular lengths, just pieces small enough for one man to drag round to the stump where they would raise the fire. To begin with it was easy, as there was enough weight in each limb to hold it steady and the compression and tension along the length was regular and predictable. As they moved down each branch, though, there came a point when more thought was required. And oak is hard wood and heavy on the saws.

They could get no more than half an hour out of the chains before they succumbed and needed sharpening, and the last five minutes of those were stern measure. It was hard, slow work, knotting their shoulders and wearing heavy on their arms. After lunch they lit the fire, Jack taking tobacco from his pipe and knocking it into the faggot of dried bracken, the colour of copper, bound around with the birch twigs he had collected on his foray. He puffed at it gently until it began to glow and turned the bracken over it. Blue smoke massed at the end, seeping out and drawing back as the fire within began to breathe. It broke free in a thin line and a crackle and he thrust it into the centre of the brash he had stacked over the stump. They watched silently, reverently, as the pyre began, adjusting the timber as the wind caught at the flames, drawing them upwards, thin and tall, frayed at the edges, leaves turning and twisting in the heat as they dried, popping noisily before taking hold, flaming orange for a few seconds in myriad points, before the ash would break free and rise on the plume of thick white smoke. Flies appeared at the edges of the pall, born as if from the smoke, and buzzed and danced at each other, enlivened and intoxicated like ancient prophets.

Oak is an alchemist, first among mages. She takes water and air and makes them solid and still, stretching out her arms in supplication to the sun who commands them stay there, for ever in tension, in opposition to the earth. She takes rock and makes of it dust, leaving it to blow in the wind or wash away in the rain, teaching it the meaning of endurance and strength.

When it was well alight they stirred themselves, trying to return their spirits to the world around them and the work in hand. Each was blinkered for a while, so far down a road of their own thought had they travelled. He sharpened his saw whilst Jack returned to drag timber round and feed the fire and Simon carried on cutting. They were too close for comfort to be working at the same time now. When he was done he refuelled and set it aside, joining Jack until Simon had blunted his saw, when they would change around. Jack had stripped from his shirt and a greyed and frayed vest encased his girth like the shell of an egg. He would have passed comment, thinking it must be the first time in ten years he had seen him so undressed, when his eyes fell on the deep scar which puckered the hollow where his collar bone reached his shoulder, with its silvered pink tail like a comet rising from his chest.

'I was daft in my youth,' Jack replied, though no question had been asked, and he tried not to smile at this, struggling with the thought of Jack as a youth, never mind Jack being daft, ever. He made do with a nod and the twitch of his mouth which he used to mean yes when he did not manage to speak. He knew nothing of Jack's former life, as he knew nothing of Simon's or Adam's, as they knew nothing of his. He had seen a stab wound once before, though, and knew the wound must have been harsh and strong-intentioned. The saw drowned the bird song and most conversation in its troubled sea of noise and they worked solidly until the pitch dropped unmistakably. Simon stopped, pulling off his helmet and wiping the sweat before it ran into his eyes.

They had held some timber back and they stacked it on to the fire whilst Jack collected the horses. It would burn through the night, and through the week, the flames eating their way along the trunk they had left uncut, until all was charcoal. It would be past supper when they got back and he was dearly hoping that Elsie had kept some food for them, great and terrible soul that she was. They were subdued and silenced on the way, listening to the songs of the woods in the early evening, speaking only when they raised two yearlings which had stopped at the stream they were to cross, one drinking, the other watching. They flicked their ears, uncertain but steady, one breath, then two, when a fish leapt clear from the water and crashed into the shallows at their feet, droplets of light spraying out from the silver sides. Startled, they turned, springing away with immediate speed, vanishing into the thicket which bore no marks of their passing. Beautiful life. Sleek and firm, full of grace and effortless power. As one the horses flicked their tails and tossed their heads and he wondered if they were jealous of the freedom. Or whether some memory of the chase was passed down the species. He was glad the dogs were in the kennels. Lucy sidled and tried to pass and Jack grabbed his rein and shouted. Such a strange noise in the gentle woodland, so foreign like the angry sound of a chainsaw, that the birds for a moment stopped, then resumed their singing. Lucy snorted on but fell into place. The fish thrashed clear of the shallows and swam on.

'Did you ever see a salmon this high?' Simon was asking, 'It must have got lost.'

'The world's gone daft,' Jack agreed.

* * *

It was Magda who had pointed out the hoof prints in the dust of the narrow track, and throughout the day she seemed restless as if waiting to see the horses that had caused them. When she rode, bareback and bareheaded, she thrilled to it. As soon as she was able, she would stir her mount to a canter then gallop down the park with her hair flailing out behind, turning tightly round a stand or a tree then back, slowing at the last minute with no apparent effort on the reins. She would ride until the horse was lathered then return it, her smile wide, the laughter flowing from her like a mountain stream. Her eyes wild with the pleasure of chasing the wind.

It was Magda who pointed out the column of smoke rising through the trees, straight and tall into the clear blue sky, until at its very tip it began to drag in the high breeze. It held her attention for a while and she might have been dancing with the way she swayed, her body rippling in S-curves, her humming low and rhythmic. Then she stopped, her arms stretched out wide before her, her fingers spread and long as if trying to reach for what she could not. Michael heard nothing but the drum of his heart beating loudly in his chest. Hypnotised by the grace of this strange sibyl, he raised a trembling hand to clear his fringe from his eyes, and wetted dry lips with his tongue. He had not felt this alive for such a time. He had forgotten the excitement of it.

It was Magda who laughed in recognition when he showed her the pictures of the maze but shook her head when he asked her where it was.

'Can you show me then?' he tried, agitated, enraged by Lucia's nudes now, more than he had ever realised.

She nodded and reached for her sandals as if expecting to set off straight away. He did not wish to leave his picture and looked from her to it. The strong fingers of root grasped the rock tightly, crushing it unrelentingly as if about to break it, furious and unappeased, determined on destruction. The rock strained back, bulging out through the gaps, trying to prise the hand apart, trying to escape. Birdsong? There was dawn chorus. He packed his things.

Magda was joyful, skipping along and leading him teasingly. Ignoring his questions and suggestions as to where it might be, enjoying her knowledge. Finally, she took his hand and led him into the maze. The air was still and close, warmed from the day's sun, still high above them. It glared from the gravel at their feet and he found himself confused by the perspective and the deep shadow of the yew hedges, like night made solid, enclosing them. Hand in hand they walked and he was glad of her steadiness to guide him, hot and febrile as he was. He could hear little but his own breathing and the pulse of life in his neck, and their soft tread, in time. She was intense, trance-like almost, concentrating on the choices to be made, seeing the paths in her memory. Her focus on the statues directed his attention to them. The erotic narrative of the sequence became explicit to him and the thought of Magda, so close, alone and unobserved, stirred him. He slipped his free hand into his pocket to cover his arousal, clearing his throat as he did so.

She reached up and covered his eyes with her cool hands, nudging him forward with her body despite his protestations and laughter, nervous now, his hands before him to guide his way. He felt himself trembling, feeling her pressure at his back, scenting the citronella and bergamot he had smoothed into her neck and shoulders. He felt the cooler air, the darkness through her fingers as they passed into the cloister, and the heat sudden and intense, assailing him as they entered the space. She released him and he gasped, gawping stupidly at the immaculate topiary, the lines razor sharp, perfect. She laughed at his wonder, a pure sound ringing out in the sanctuary, and he turned to her speechless, smiling widely.

She had one last surprise and took his hand again, leading him over to the table. His head spun in the pattern of the stars, set as if in nothing, a total absence of light. He touched it to confirm its real presence, running his hand out over it, tracing Orion, entranced. He straightened again, finding her close to him, and kissed her spontaneously in gratitude, making her blink and smile in surprise, her laugh nervous and her eyes downcast. Then, despite himself, he kissed her again, aroused as she moved to free herself from his arms.

13

The Hall was quiet as they rode up the drive, the gravel crunching under the hooves. The brightness of the borders which ran away from the steps along the front of the building was softened by the evening light, giving a greater depth of colour to the individual blooms. They were at their full height now and danced gently to the music of the wind. It would be fine, avoiding accident, for the return of the Palmers. They carried on round to the stable block, thinking they would put the horses in the stalls for the night rather than bother to turn them out.

Suzie was waiting for them, sat on the mounting block with Adam, touchingly close, his arm around her. They dismounted and stretched, tethering the horses and unbuckling the girths, prepared to chat in that way which puts an end to the day.

'Don't you worry about those,' Suzie was saying. 'Adam and me will do 'em. Elsie wants to see you all 'bout somethin' or other.' Nothing in her tone suggested anything odd and Adam and herself were relaxed in manner, easy in each other's company. Adam exchanged looks with his boss, however, from behind Suzie's head, which said enough.

'Don't bother putting the saws away tonight. I'll collect them tomorrow and fettle them first thing.' Keep everything normal, he was thinking. 'Then get yourselves away and have some fun. Good man.' Adam's look was not about having fun; he recognised the signs, the burden of unwanted knowledge.

'What was for pudding?' Jack was asking Suzie.

'Rhubarb crumble.'

'But we ate all of it,' Adam butted in gamely.

When they entered the refectory Alex and Elsie were on either side of a table, a bottle of whiskey and glasses between them. Elsie rose straightaway, casting 'I'll bring your dinner' as she disappeared into the kitchen. Like an attentive host at a party, Alex poured them each a drink and strained to the nearest water jug in case they wanted it.

They listened in silence as they ate. It was soon told. To their credit they refrained from the supposition which so often blighted such events, keeping the story tight, brutal. Just Magda bursting from the maze, wall-eyed and running, her dress torn, her breasts bared. Ben gathering her up despite the screams and the greater pain of the silences as she sank her teeth deep into his shoulder, worrying at it until it flowed red.

Jack was in danger of crushing his glass in pieces, his knuckles whitened around it, as he took it in. Simon too was beyond words.

'How do we know it wasn't Ben?'

'He's one of yours and you ask that?' Alex was outraged.

'I think it is safe to say Ben wouldn't have the interest.'

It took him a moment to follow Elsie's meaning, but the hand that strayed to quieten Alex confirmed it. Now that he thought, Ben had never been associated with any of the ladies.

'Adam knows. Who else?'

'Just Adam. I sent him to watch.'

'And?'

'Adam said he had a strange smile on his face. Nothing more.'

'The man's cracked.' Simon had recovered his voice.

'I'll fucking kill the fucker!' Jack raged. Death lay in his eyes. The clear grey of the one, the darkness of the other, monstrous somehow.

He let the violence of the words subside, looking from one to another before he spoke, almost inaudibly.

'No, Jack.'

'Who's going to fucking stop me – you? So that you can keep fucking his fucking wife? How dare he touch her? To . . .'

'That opinion does not flatter you, my friend.' His low interjection, so calm now, the menace of ultra-violence raising the hairs on all their necks.

'Sit yourself down Jack. How is she?' His voice was thick with sadness. She was the important one here.

'Like she was when you found her when she had found Sam.' Alex took over the telling, as Elsie was avoiding his look. He had thought his business with Lucia was widely known.

'Sedated?'

'Not yet. It . . . Well, we don't even know if she's hearing us.' His eyes welled with tears also, and he looked away.

'Good. I'll take a look. Perhaps there is something I can do.'

Simon and Jack were shifting on their benches and he could feel himself losing this.

'I'll tell you a story. One of you knows it already.' His eyes flicked to Elsie's face to reassure her, *not that one,* as he poured more whiskey for them all. His voice was so quiet they strained to hear.

'In my life before I had a friend. A good friend, my closest. He betrayed . . . trust, in a manner similar to the one before us, not as serious perhaps or perhaps more so, as we do not know the full truth – an abuse of his strength, though. I thought about it and decided I would hit him, just the once. To show him that strength is not secure. Except, when I had hit him, I found that it was not enough, so I hit him again. And again. And when he went down, I followed him.' He sipped his whiskey, lowering his eyes and breathing deeply before going on. 'I beat him until the shit burst out of him. And it wasn't enough. For a week, ten days at most, I felt calmer. Then my anger lived again, flowing in my blood, the heat from a fever, giving me no peace. I considered what I could do to satisfy it.' His eyes picked them out again, one

141

by one. 'His death would not have been enough for me at that time . . . and no amount of pain you inflict on the fool will change the past, or bring you satisfaction, or alter his nature.'

'We can't do nothing. Is that what you are suggesting?' Simon was trembling as he spoke, outraged.

'No, of course not . . . But there are other ways.'

'I'm still for the beating.'

He held up a hand. 'This is mine, Jack.' He turned to Simon. 'Are you getting many rats in the barns?'

'A fair few, yes.'

'I'll take two tomorrow. Live. I don't want this talked of and I don't want him touched.'

'What are you going to do to him?' Jack was not yet convinced.

'It's probably better you don't know. Just know that he will suffer.'

There was a silence of foreboding; they had never seen him like this, dead-eyed and cold. Elsie brought the meeting to a close – 'Until tomorrow then' – and she raised her glass to seal the business.

He leaned back against the wall, unseeing, as the others departed. When the door clicked shut Elsie reached for the hand which lay curled on the table top. He grasped hers hard, his eyes clouding now with tears.

'I thought you would tell them about Sam. You need to, you know.'

'Sam was well loved and rightly. They don't need to see what I saw.'

'It eats at you.' She was firm now.

'No. They cannot know.'

She watched, concerned, as his breathing became laboured. 'Listen . . .'

'What is it about her, Elsie? Why . . . do they . . . do . . . this . . . to her?' His voice failed entirely and he made for her other hand but she snatched it away, rising and turning in one moment so that he was left looking at her back. Her voice was cold water to a drunk.

'If you had told the others this wouldn't have happened.'

'I've been watching him . . .'

'We all could have watched him! But you are so insular. And now this self-pity!' She could be withering when she wanted something.

* * *

Michael felt replete, satisfied. He set a bath running and wandered through to the upper lounge, pausing to examine his *Birth of Magda*, or *Death of a Maiden*, he was undecided as to which, on his way to the drinks, nodding and appraising before passing on. His plump tongue emerged from his mouth, moist and pink, lazily exploring his lips, leaving a glistening trail as it slid over the bottom, the tip pressing in before rising to the top. It withdrew and his white teeth closed over it. He unstoppered the cut decanter of cognac, pouring a generous amount into the balloon and sipping it cold, considering. His tongue swabbed the traces away. He lit his last cigarette and although the annoyance registered, it carried no weight.

He started to undress as he wandered around the room, unbuttoning his shirt, the sides parting like split skin as the pressure was released, his pale belly revealed. He drifted through to the bedroom, remembering the mirror behind the door, and stood in contemplation of himself, absently rubbing at his jaw, which was tender from its meeting with Magda's head the day before. He had never been happy with his legs, overly thin with a strange disproportion of the thigh and shin. They were better, the exploration of the estate had helped to tone them, and he could trace a line of muscle above the knee and a little recess which had not been there previously. He held his cigarette in his lips to free up a hand and he poked at his stomach, his fingers sinking in, not meeting with resistance, the flesh closing over and hiding his nails.

143

He paused to draw and sip before running a flatter hand round the curve of it, overhanging his pants and up to his left breast, drawn by the slight shadow it was casting. He cupped it in his hand feeling the weight of it and the firmness of its conical mound topped by the mean little nipple, a pink stain on the dough-white skin. His arms were thin and striped different shades, darker at the hands and fading to the shoulders and looking left behind somehow, now that the legs had improved. He had good teeth, though, and he bared them, even and white, and he had always been pleased with his mouth which he considered sensuously full. His complexion was clear, if ruddier than it had been before he had spent so much time outdoors, and his hair was always bright and well behaved. He ran a hand through it, comforting himself with its abundance.

He knew he looked better when dressed, when his shirts would modify his lines, hanging widely enough from his broad-shouldered frame to accommodate his burgeoning mass, the product of too much food and wine. He loved his wine, though, but thought perhaps he should cut down, if only because some of his trousers had been getting tight. He sipped again at his cognac, warmer now from its cradling in his hand, his tongue revelling in the complex flavours, the smell of it captured by his nose, so pleasing to look at as the light came through it, the oily way in which it coated the crystal as he twirled it.

He poached himself in the hottest bath he could tolerate until he was a glowing pink all over, warm and relaxed, and revelling in his freedom. When he was done he poured himself a second large glass and descended to the kitchen in search of the particularly fine cheese he had procured from the Hall. A memory of his resolve cautioned his hand as he hefted the knife, and he sliced a small piece, quickly followed by another so that the total was more than the one large piece he had intended originally. It went so well with the alcohol, though, that he was even tempted just to straighten it up a little. Thus fortified he retired for the night.

The darkness of the bedroom seemed particularly comforting, he had not noticed just how harsh the bulb in there was before, and he settled himself sleepily. After what seemed like hours of trying to lie still and composed, imitating sleep in the hope it might come, interspersed with tossing and turning, suddenly uncomfortable and aware unpleasantly of his limbs, he switched on the bedside light, wincing at the brightness and shielding his eyes as he reached for his watch. Very little time had passed. Feeling thirsty with a thick tongue, dry and hot, he rose for a glass of water, flicking on the landing light as he passed, and feeling assailed by it. It bore into his head at the temples, making him squint accusingly at this unexpected source of pain.

He stood over the bowl of the toilet, thinking he might as well whilst he was up, holding it there, not really concentrating as he smoothed the back of his head. Despite his desire he could not manage until after ardent minutes of desperate will, a dark streak of piss burnt its way out of him and he sighed with relief. It felt like the nasty little infection he had picked up at college but he was too befuddled to think about it properly. He drank some water, swallowing hard and wondering whether he had dozed off without realising and had snored, open-mouthed and stupid.

When sleep came it gripped him hard, immersing him in violent dreams of fires, everywhere fires. He wanted to run but each way he turned the flames sprang up to the height of him. Though still a long way off they were moving towards him. He searched the sky but his eyes were blind to all except the flames, which burned his eyes and hurt his head. He saw a gap and made towards it but his limbs now were heavy and reluctant. He fought on through the thickness that caught at his feet and ankles, he could not see below his knees, and thought it was his chance. He was slowing, though, the ground was rising up it seemed, or he was in a forest he could not see and which did not obscure the fires, because the very air was solidifying around him and he was clawing through it, flailing his arms. He was stopped, panting open-mouthed though it hurt so much, the air so hot and rasping over his tongue. Prickly heat coursed through him, welling up under his arms and in his throat. The gap closed and the fires drew towards him. He could not move, his arms were pinned to his sides and it did not seem to matter how hard he tried, he could not close his eyes. There was the sound of someone running, or more than one, out beyond the flames which he realised now were silent.

His pounding heart felt fit to burst deep in the tightened cage of ribs. He knew he had been asleep and the dream memory was heavy upon him. Still he could not move and a great weight was on his chest, making his breathing laboured. Pain punctured his right shoulder and shot down his side, and he heard himself cry out. There was laughter in return, somewhere above him where he could not see and running steps again, back and forth, below him or perhaps to the side, if he could only turn his head to look.

When morning came he awoke. He was lain on his back with his right arm tucked beneath him, his hand under his buttocks. He dragged it out, feeling the pain of returning blood and rubbing to disperse the pins and needles. His foot was caught, wrapped twice around in the sheet, the covers in chaos, bunched on top of him. He reached for the glass of water to refresh his parched mouth but it and the lamp were smashed on to the floor, the dark shadow of the water visible on the rug. He rolled properly on to his back, feeling like death.

It was a good while before he roused himself, the night sat heavily upon him still, but the lying down became uncomfortable at last. He ran himself a bath, wishing to cleanse the profuse sweat away, but felt little compunction to get into it. The water seemed to take for ever to settle and he eyed it suspiciously before lowering himself delicately. He could not endure it for long, it felt hotter than he had thought at first, and he was uncomfortably pink. The cramps which were shooting down his right side subsided, though, and that in itself was a relief.

The day was overcast, serried ranks of clouds rolling out from behind the mountain like waves approaching the shore. He considered the dark underbelly of each row and the lighter troughs which divided them. He had got better at reading the weather since coming here but this was perplexing and he suspected it might rain later. The light was kind, though, and perfect for the finishing touches he wished to make down by the lake. It did not matter really if he only worked a half day, especially if it did rain, not that he thought anybody was keeping tabs on him, that had just been a whim, and he definitely did not feel right.

He collected his food and waited at the edge of the lawn for Magda, whom he was keen to see again after a day without, to smooth things over between them, to try again, more slowly perhaps. He surveyed the park as he did so, marvelling at the changes. The meadow was thick and lush now and so studded with buttercups that it was as equally golden as green. There was an heraldic quality to the colours, so vibrant and bold, and he knew that if he were to paint it accurately he would be accused of medievalism. Fascinating, the way the very ground seemed to glow in the diffuse light, so brightly without being vulgar. Raised as he was on the terrace, he could look down over the scene and he noticed how the buttercups disappeared around the trees, evenly, to a distance of about half again the radius of the canopy. He shook his head in wonder at this, reminding himself that it was hurting. He sipped water from the flask, thinking he really must insist that the flask be rinsed properly. Magda was nowhere to be seen and, growing bored and impatient with her, he set off alone.

The day was growing warmer and felt to him like thunder. He was reassured by this consciousness as it would explain his head, which was always bad before a storm. He unbuttoned his shirt further, hurting again as the pain haunted his right shoulder and thinking how stupid he had been to have slept so. He remembered troubled dreams but not their content and thought perhaps Lucia had been right to go away when she did, before the isolation grew oppressive. She was free to come and go as she pleased, though, whereas he was a hired hand at the end of the day, indentured labour or as good as until his lordship saw fit to put in an appearance and have his bloody portrait painted. He knew in his heart that he would be thinking differently if Magda were with him; if his desire to continue their little conversation had not been frustrated. The trees were pretty at least and his heart warmed to the familiar subject as he set down his box.

He worked well again, emphasising the conflict between rock and root, imbuing the subject with a tension of which he had not thought he was capable. It became a powerful picture. The composure of it was essentially primitive but that complemented the emotion of the struggle. The tonal similarities expressed something of the common nature of the materials and through that a pointlessness in the conflict.

He began to feel jaded after lunch. The cloud had been swept away by the increasing breeze, leaving the day gloriously bright and strangely painful. The sun was too hot and hurt his eyes and head. He was simply unable to shake the headache today. The wind was raising peaks on the lough, which lapped the shore with increasing frequency and irritation. The noise began to madden and he could not help but keep looking at the waves, wishing they would be still. He stopped and mopped at his brow with the tail of his shirt and could not begin again.

Once home, he went from room to room drawing the curtains to shut out the light and start to cool the house. He cleaned his brushes with even less pleasure than normal, barely able to see in the dimness whether the solvent was running clear or not, before setting them aside. Listlessly he filled a glass with water and slumped at the table, resting his forehead against the cool, smooth wood. Its solidity reassured and brought relief, a fixed place for his spinning head to be.

He had sat feeling tired and sipping water, as much as he could manage at once, until he could bear the smell no longer and thought he had identified it. He uncovered the cheese, eyeing it suspiciously, fighting down the wave of nausea which assailed him. He bent over it, averting his eyes and giving the smallest of sniffs to capture some aroma. He gagged and snatched it up, enclosing it in the wrapping so as not to contaminate his hands. He strode for the door, holding the cheese out and away from himself, breathing shallowly through clenched teeth. The late afternoon sun was bright and savage still, the day full of life. He shielded his eyes with his free hand, pausing for a moment, at a loss as to what to do with the offending article. On a post a blackbird twisted and bobbed before rising tall to sing its beautiful song.

'What are you fucking happy about?' he screamed at the bird, who fell silent and bobbed again. Then with a wave of anger he did not understand, he hurled the cheese at the bird, who flew from it, clicking in disapproval. The cheese ruptured on the post, cleaving to it in a broken mass of white skin and pale, yellowed flesh. Slowly it began to run, liquefying in the heat, a large drop freeing itself and falling to earth. He spat on the ground, a thick, mucus-rich emission, before turning and slamming the door on the world. The noise split his head afresh and he resumed his vigil of the tabletop.

The watcher on the hill set down his binoculars and gave each of the dogs who sat beside him a stroke. He had seen all that he needed to for the moment and turned for home. He would return later to see what the night might bring.

It was evening and morning, another day. Michael woke suddenly and ran for the bathroom. Diarrhoea convulsed him and he sat for a long while before he considered it safe, washing before returning to bed. He had finished the last of his lunch, the Magda portion, for supper. He had not felt up to eating much really. The chicken pie which had been so nice at lunchtime still tasted good even if the pastry had sweated slightly in the heat of the day. The pâté had likewise had a finer hour but it was beautifully seasoned and not too smooth. He could not abide smooth pâté. He had toasted some of the coarse-grained bread on the top of the range and spread the paste upon it thickly, slice after slice, until the stoneware pot it had come in was clean. Having forgotten to collect any wine he sipped cognac, which cut through the richness very effectively if overwhelming the flavour a little. He had searched the house for cigarettes but knew before he began that it would most likely be futile, and went to bed dissatisfied. Sleep had been elusive for a second night.

Now, as he lay in contemplation of the ceiling, he remembered the pie and judged it a mistake to have inflicted it on his stomach after the disruption it had suffered from the cheese. He would have to eat plainly for a couple of days to cleanse his system. Cleansing or not, he could kill for a cigarette, and the headache, which he attributed now to withdrawal, pounded as if to remind him. More dreams of fire had troubled him through the night and he imagined he could smell the smoke still in his nostrils, acrid and thick. And he was sure that he had woken again, his chest tight and that pain like claws in his right shoulder. There had been whispered voices beyond where he could see, and footsteps.

He rallied after a while and wandered over to the Hall, relieved to make it safely with his troubled bowel. The staff he passed on the way were as friendly as they ever had been but they did seem to be staring at him more than was usual. He thought when he set off that his shirt was long enough to cover him but now he suspected that they could see. But he could not help it, his balls ached, hard and swollen, tight to his body, and he kept trying to draw them down with his hand. They were ugly fools anyway. Even the cook, whom he had fantasised over, had a hardness to her demeanour which soured her beauty, cruel-looking bitch. He hated having to ask her the favour of some special food, and tried really hard not to get irritated. He could hear his voice rising, in volume and pitch, and still she looked at him contemptuously with that satisfied mouth and those arrogant eyes. The desire to spit in her haughty face gripped him and it was only the sound of the door opening which pre-empted him. The gardener had come in.

'We need to talk about vegetables . . . and fruit. If you've finished.' He held Michael's gaze commandingly, assessing the symptoms of the toxin with which he had laced the cognac. Michael blinked and lowered his widely dilated eyes to the floor, steadying himself on the bench as he did so, his head lurching violently.

'Yes. Send the food over. I can't move far at the moment.' And with that he barged to the door, trying to shoulder the gardener as he passed but missing somehow, having to make do with a slam.

'Well?' she asked, turning her eyes on him.

'Well, he's brighter than I thought,' he answered neutrally.

'He'll get worse, do you mean? I thought that was pretty bad.' Her heart was beating quickly still. She had not approved of this plan when she had had the detail explained, and having to suffer the consequences angered her.

'Probably, yes . . . But no. I mean, he's more intelligent than I realised. The beautiful lady has more effect on the intelligent.'

They looked at each other for long moments as she tried to search him. He discerned her hurt.

'Are you all right? What was he screaming about anyway?' And his voice carried all the care he felt for her.

'He was accusing me of poisoning him with an under-cooked chicken pie. He wants boiled rice, steamed vegetables, that sort of thing, for a couple of days.' She shrugged, picking up a cloth and wiping the surface of the clean counter.

'Good. I'll give him one more day then antidote tomorrow.'

'So that he thinks he was right?'

'Aye. Then I'll begin again.'

'Be careful.'

'He'll feel hell for a few days, nothing more.'

'Be careful – for you, I mean.'

He shrugged his lack of consequence, eyes downcast, not seeing the hand that swung out, striking hard, her ring splitting his lip as it coursed across his face. He gasped, astonished.

'You matter to some of us, even if you don't matter to yourself.' She turned and left him standing. A heaviness settled within him. He could not say that he had wanted any of this.

* * *

Dear Anna,

I have been in touch with the solicitors and they are sorting out the papers so that the house in Thorncliffe can be signed over to you. It is tenanted at the moment and I admit I don't know when the tenancy expires, it will be in the details, though. Do with it as you please. When it is completed they will notify my family who hopefully will not trouble you. They will have no proper grounds to trouble you, anyway. My uncle signed it to me in his lifetime and dealt with all the legal subtleties then. So just tell them.

I'm sorry I didn't do it before. I haven't needed the money and you could have had the benefit. I think for a long time I did not know whether this was a permanent situation. I will not leave here now.

We had a run out the other day and I realised just how well I know the place. Every stream we crossed held memories and associations, I recognised rocks and particular trees. More widely too – particular land forms, the fall of a hill or the way it frames the sky. The light at different times of day or the cloud forming when the air is warm and the wind turns to the north-west. The wildflowers I expect to see in field or woodland and those which catch me by surprise because I have been inattentive. I would not say I understand it, more that I and this land have come to an understanding. It makes sense to me. I know I will not return from here now, the thought of life elsewhere is not tolerable.

I remember once you asked if I was happy here. I'm not sure that I was, and I know that then I did not think it was possible, certainly not in the way I imagined when we were young and knew little. I have times of deep satisfaction when a job is well done. There is a fellowship which arises between us when we are working hard at something. It makes the job lighter, which is a reward in itself, but it runs deeper than that. I have moments when the beauty of the world is almost too much to bear and I ache for it. I take pleasure in my food. But I am a scarred man and I underestimated the extent of that damage. And I would still rather be scarred, knowing what I know, than have that knowledge taken away or to have learnt it and remained untouched by it. I keep myself busy and that is the main thing.

Still, this is my life now, for better or worse. I share the sensibilities of those around me and that carries enough acceptance to tolerate the inevitable differences. I am freer than I would be elsewhere, and you know that was always important to me. Although, even here, I have needed to act at times for the perceived good of the community in ways I doubt the wisdom of. Inevitable, I suppose.

Regards to Patrick

Love S x

14

It was the day of preparation; the evening of return. They had never been away for such a long period before and this uncharacteristic absence had led to whisperings of supposed discontent and rumours of sale. They grew as if from nothing and their spectre haunted even those who gave them no credence, as the agitation of the believers became infectious. It was a strange phenomenon, as if however perfect the world, some have a need for strife. It was not enough to have a place and a purpose of one's own, to be trusted to acquit oneself without supervision or interference, or at least without more interference than could be reasonably expected. To find satisfaction through that work and at the end of each day to eat and drink the fruit of good labour. It was not enough to live peacefully among friends united by a common decision and purpose. To have homes and warmth, comforts and luxuries. It was not enough to have arts and artistry, music and dancing and singing, games and good health. To be immersed in the infinitely variable beauty of the world, at sunrise a revelation, at sunset apotheosis. To walk beneath that sun in the fullness of strength, feeling the good earth beneath your feet and the living air in your lungs. To love the rain, the welcome cleansing of the sky, feeding the earth and bringing it life. To have the mind expand, reaching out to the wooded slopes of the hill behind the lough, trying to understand the whole of it, the endlessly shifting sea of leaves in so many shades of green, each tree a different resonance as the wind stirred it, from the steadfastness of the yew to the yielding of the poplar. To see the play of the light as the air moved over the waters raising waves, or its stillness, grey and hard, before the first flash of lightning announced a storm.

It was not enough and he did not understand it, this appetite for purposeless trouble, a psychic parasite that imitated life in order to destroy it more effectively. As if trouble did not come looking even for those who did not desire it.

He threw his half-smoked cigarette on to the gravel and ground it beneath the ball of his foot. Smoking did not please him any more but he feared what he would be like without it. His body knew the patterns of action required and their stimuli. It was a comfort to reach for the pouch and roll the yielding leaf between his thumb and forefinger, feeling the moisture, awakening the complex scent, earthy and sharp. To breathe it in on crisp winter mornings and to smell it on the frosted air, or through warm summer evenings, mixing it with the scent of stocks and of the grass as the dew begins to settle. He would have to relearn so much. How would he occupy himself when asked for an opinion he did not wish to give and was stalling for time? Or when unwelcome thoughts preyed on his mind, his hand reaching to his pocket as he remembered her huddled in the corner of the room, her knees drawn up and wrapped tightly in her arms. Her hair dulled and greasy looking, although the girls washed and brushed it every day, enduring the frozen limbs and tortured sobs which broke their own hearts. Memories of his grandmother kept surfacing in his mind, a shadow against the white hospital sheets, twisted by the stroke. But she was old and had had her time. Magda was still beginning. It seemed cruel fate indeed to be recovered from the trauma of Sam only to be cast back. Really, it was too much for a body to bear. Her eyes so far away and brittle-seeming at the edges. Beautiful, more beautiful than ever but fragile like ancient glass. He ran his tongue along the edge of the paper and sealed another cigarette. His lighter flashed, the settled flame hardly visible in the brightness of the day. He looked down through hot, reddened eyes at the broken fingernails of his dirty hands. What would they do at these times if they weren't smoking a cigarette?

The futility of his strength was heavy upon him. Strength of body and strength of heart, of all their hearts. Strength which had failed for a second time to protect that which was most precious, though nobody could have predicted the first. He did not know the darkened paths down which Magda travelled in the labyrinth of her mind, nor how exactly they could help to lead her out. It was worse this time, that was certain; she had shown no improvement in a week, none whatsoever. It was all they could do to stop her fading, to keep at least the biological functions alive; a little food, some water, long hours of patience, coaxing and soothing, and watching. Not knowing the full cause was a hard sentence, inviting the mind to speculation. Elsie had reported bruising to Magda's arms above the elbows, as if she had been gripped tightly, but no other outward signs. Perhaps Jack was right when he said to touch was crime enough.

He knew the darkened paths down which Michael travelled, leading him further, waking or sleeping, forging a hideous landscape with the drug in which the mind could not rest and the body find no peace. He had been amazed by the amount the artist was drinking, underestimating that as he had his intelligence. The dosage had been fine but aggravated by the alcohol in that quantity, making it unpredictable. When he had entered at night, knowing Michael would be paralysed, knowing that his footsteps on the stairs would enter the dreams, dreams of attack, dreams of thieves, dreams of laughing demons whose claws would dig so cruelly as they sat upon his chest, he had looked through the pictures and notebooks. The sketches in the books were excellent – Michael was a truly talented draughtsman, and improving as time passed – recorded so neatly in full at the bottom of each page, the time and location, in a script even and neat. A record of his movements around the estate. A record of the growth of his obsession.

He had made a detailed study of Magda, as that was surely who these hands belonged to, that line of the collar bone, the curve of a breast. He was not concerned that Michael had seen these things, it was common practice to swim naked in the lough, and it was known they had swum together. He thought he might be retrojecting an intention where none was present, but the sketches did seem to have a fascination with detail – the texturing of skin, and a movement in the composition which directed the eye time and again to where it did not need to be. It was beyond anatomical study. The line drawing of her head and shoulders terminating in the curve of her breasts was erotic without apology and he found himself sickened by the motive. Beautiful pictures, though, transcendent really; it was only knowing the subject and what might have happened that mired the rest.

Some coarse drawings of hideous, distorted faces were scattered about with no order and he knew them to be the product of the sickness. They were exceptional, nightmare images steeped in revulsion. They made him think of Oscar Wilde and of Anna's words of 'gas attack'. An ironic smile marked his face grimly at the thought he might have done the man a favour. Truly ugly pictures, transcendent all the same.

The finished tree studies had shown improvement too but a progressive, reasoned improvement as Michael learned to look and see, and had discovered his method of representation. He knew that if all the pictures were lined up on a long enough wall, in chronological order, that a narrative of Michael's own development would be told. It was seamless from one picture to the next, barely incremental 'betterness'. Yet the difference between the first series and the most recent was extraordinary. The latter had a different quality, a life, an intelligence. They engaged the very spirit of the viewer and not just the eye. It was like observing the evolution of life itself.

When he discovered the picture of Magda and saw the life within that, no matter how twisted it was with its naïve sadism of the sexually complacent, he remembered how much had been lost. He looked at it for what seemed like an age, trying to empathise with the mind which had created it. He understood her charisma; the stunning compulsion of her beauty, which had been painted very well, if truth be told. The allure of a true innocent with a gentle soul, devoid of malice too. But to do that to it. The more he looked at it the more vile he felt as if infected by its intent, until, angered by its presumption, he looked no more. He found no proof of guilt, not that he had expected to, really – there would hardly be a signed confession. Not that it mattered any more: the man had suffered now whatever and that was irreversible.

His cigarette finished, he bent over the machine and pulled the starter cord, the engine churning into life. It would be a long day of grass cutting under a hot sun, though he had stripped to his shorts and would risk the flies. The oblivion of the noise would be welcome, though, as he neither wished to speak or to be spoken to as yet. The conundrum of Magda occupied him still and, to a lesser extent, how to explain Michael's behaviour to Lord and Lady Palmer if he was not sufficiently recovered by night time. He suspected that some of the effects might prove permanent.

He had intended to cut the grass on the previous day but rain had stopped play for the second time that week. They had managed to get it measured up and pegged but that was all. It would now be a struggle to finish and get recovered for the evening but it could not be avoided. He was working down the sides of the drive, cutting three widths of the machine to tidy the edge and emphasise the meadow flowers in the grass left long beyond. Jim and Adam followed behind, cutting tracks out into the long grass, tracks with larger terminal circles. The grass had to be removed and they had walked miles by lunchtime, behind the mowers and back and forth to the trailer to empty the grass boxes. It was not over-heavy, though, and a light breeze was providing relief from the heat of the sun, making it bearable.

Ben and Simon followed after, lending a hand as need

demanded. They cut circles of turf from the centre of each terminal circle, lifting it carefully so as not to tear it, open-structured as it was with the different plants. They set the pieces into the longer grass for restoration a week or so later, when all was cleared away. When that was done they brought kindling and timber, enough to make a neat, conical fire in the centre of each clearing with provision to restack it once. They had done this for years and knew the amount needed for a six-hour fire without thinking, judging the size of the fires so that they had sufficient mass to sustain them without setting the surrounding sward ablaze. In many ways it was a daft tradition; the light of the evening lasted so long at this time of year that looking north at midnight revealed a sky not yet dark. Morning followed swiftly after, perhaps just four hours of true night. Still, it looked spectacular and helped to bridge the darkness, carrying the party over and giving energy when souls began to flag.

When he had finished the verges he began to cut a path through the front field to the main fire site. The others joined him when they were done and together they cut an area large enough for the entire staff to gather round the main fire, with room for trestles, and dancing, and drinking. At least there a trailer of timber could be brought and tipped directly on to the bared earth, being arranged less delicately as the greater space permitted.

The pressure of the work kept their minds from Lord Palmer's return that evening and it was only as they stopped, sipping the lemonade which Alex had brought out to them, and handing round the slices of dense ginger cake, refuelling, that the excitement caught up with them. He could see now that which he had been blind to; Alex and Ben standing close, exchanging furtive glances laden with care. A tragedy among tragedies that even here, in Inchnamactaire, they had to pretend. It was one of the finest nights of their social calendar, limited as it was in the small community. It marked the beginning of a quiet month on the estate, when more time could be spent taking advantage of the good weather, to swim in the lough or fish, climb the hills or ride out beyond the demesne to the coast. It was a time for coming together, spending time with particular friends, slow times of pleasure when the details of the work could be left behind.

Even Elsie managed time away from the kitchen, despite cooking for the family. He regretted he would not see more of her this year, his time being taken by Lucia. It would have been different anyway with Magda not fit. The three of them used to ride out to the far side of the lough, where a raised promontory provided an excellent diving platform. They were like a strange family on those days, taking a picnic and sitting on the soft grass to eat it, enjoying each other's company without expectation, constrained by their chaperone. They had been lovers when he first came to the estate and he was glad of it. He was glad too when they had ceased to be, their friendship growing too precious to be risked.

Alex brought other comfort than the cake and lemonade, offering torches left over from a previous year as way-markers, buying the time that they would have spent on more fires for help with moving tables. It was easily agreed and the change of work renewed the energy of the workers. It would not take long with so many hands and he would excuse his boys from further duties when it was done, as they had had the heaviest and hottest work and needed time to cool down, bathe, and recover for the evening.

He took himself off on one last tour of the garden, just to be sure, though he imagined he would probably get up early and have another look, as they would not manage anything themselves until tomorrow. The paths were all clear of weeds, the edges trimmed, and the gravel raked. He knew Ben would curse him for putting a line of footsteps in those which had not been walked upon from the day before. The hedges were line-straight and had regrown sufficiently to cover the one or two indiscretions. He used his secateurs to trim back any adventurous top shoots which had not been caught by the machines and had taken the opportunity to grow away vigorously, inserting the cuttings into the body of the hedge where they would not be seen. The border displays were all fine, combining maturity with undiminished colour although he noticed with annoyance that the slugs had discovered the *Hosta sieboldiana*, perforating its leaves and distorting the flower spikes. He detoured to the shed to recover a trap and some bait, laying it at the base of the clump, hidden by the mass of leaves. No point allowing them another free night of dining. Elsewhere a strand of Perle d'Azure had come adrift from its support and was waving at him from the far end of the grass path. He tied it in with the twine he carried in his pocket, cutting close to the knot with the razor-sharp knife he had with him always. He stepped off the border, settling the soil over his footprint with a shuckle of his hand, before straightening and looking down the length of the display from his full height. It would all be fine. Everybody had worked well this year, for which, considering everything, he was well pleased. He would see that they were rewarded.

His last call was the maze; the informal areas being allowed to be informal and not subject to the same scrutiny. He collected the hounds, who as ever were joyful at their liberation, and headed in. The same rigour of maintenance was evident and he knew he must give special thanks to Adam who had spent the previous couple of days there. The grass of the cloister was magnificent. Adam, it seemed, had had a flight of fancy when he cut it. Each of the quarters was cut in arcs parallel to the circumference of the star table, so that the lines radiated out like ripples in a pool, light and dark alternately, lessening the formality of the space and genuinely cheering. He thought perhaps Adam had been trying to exorcise the ghost of what was assumed to have happened here, but whatever the cause, it was a terrific result.

He walked towards the table and was caught out when the

dogs ran past him and on into the corner of shadow, their hackles raised and their legs stiff, drawing themselves up at the front, and looking back to him for guidance. He frowned and passed the table and when his line of sight cleared their backs, he could see, huddled in the corner, his arms raised as if to protect himself, Michael. He called the dogs to heel and they settled themselves each side of him, still bristling and growling in their throats, though, waiting to be reassured.

'Are you waiting for someone?' he asked, genuinely curious.

'Dogs, they're just dogs.' Michael spoke as much to himself as anyone.

'Of course, you've met them before . . . What did you think they were?'

Michael looked at him squarely for the first time. 'Oh I don't know. They seemed bigger.'

'I heard you've been under the weather. I trust you are feeling better.' He hoped genuinely that he was, as the treatment had only been intended as a warning, an association his subconscious would make if he was tempted again.

'Mostly, thank you,' came the reply, but he noticed the nervousness with which it was delivered and the facial spasms, and he knew there was still poison in his system. A shiftiness lingered in his eyes too, a complication, as if the effort of telling the truth always seemed greater than the casual lie.

'Good. Will you be there tonight?'

'Tonight?' Michael looked startled.

'We celebrate the return of Lord and Lady Palmer. There'll be music and, well, drinking.'

'I don't know, I'll see how I feel.'

He nodded in response, still trying to gauge the extent of the recovery. 'Of course. Tell me, did you discover this for yourself?' And he waved a hand indicating the cloister.

'Ugh . . . no . . . Lucia showed me it.'

'Hmm.' And with that he was gone. He was sure that Michael was lying but in such a way that he could defend himself if challenged. More intelligent than he had thought, though, and of course he would be, or why would Lucia have had anything to do with him?

Michael gnawed at his lip for a while longer, staring at the space where the gardener had been, black and featureless with the sun behind him, tall and threatening, just a voice, malevolent and intent on violence. He remembered him with that hare and the look he had given him then. He needed out now, the thought of another day, never mind a month, filled him with horror. He could barely face going back to that house with its strange noises. If only he had neighbours, or at least a lock upon the door. How could they sleep with no security? Or Lucia, if she would just come back. Just another body in the house would help. Anything at all.

* * *

The flare went up from the brow of the hill as the car was spotted, and it hung red and low in the valley, staining the sunset with its slowly fading light. It was answered by another, discharged from the roof out over the front field, changing the sky and bloodying the grass as the silver car swept up, the drive-side fires glowing in its paint work, reflecting from the windows. Lord Palmer brought it to a halt at the base of the steps with the staff stood about expectantly. A minute may have passed, the tension mounting, as they all stared at the darkened windows of the car. The door opened, sucking on its seal, a light glowing within. Lord Palmer stepped out, standing tall and smiling broadly at them all, breathing in the air and adjusting to 'home'. Before anybody could respond to his greeting, other doors popped open, disgorging Lady Palmer and Amelia. There was a collective intake of breath at the sight of the young lady, not seen for nine months because of being away at school and the disruption over Christmas. The change upon her was extraordinary. She was passing into womanhood, no matter the sixteen years; tall and willowy and knowing. She flicked her head to displace the tresses of black curls which fell over her face, the gesture so reminiscent of her half-sister that Elsie was not alone in feeling the pang of grief. She came round the rear of the car to her mother's side, a child again in the presence of all those who had known her for so long.

Michael had been roused by the first flare and had stumbled out, thinking it might do for a distraction, a balm to the cabin fever he was suffering. He was distressed to see the valley below him alight as he reached the top of the hill. He shambled down, falling twice on the wet grass and marking the knees of his trousers. He made for the largest fire, where it was clear all the people had congregated, making his way distastefully through the tunnel of flares, the fear rising from within and beading his forehead with sweat. When he reached the clearing he cast around, at a loss as to whom to approach as they all seemed absorbed in their own groups. He saw her with her back to him and made towards her, weaving slightly from the bottle of red he had consumed on an empty stomach before venturing out. Impulsively he called her name, realising as she turned that it was not whom he thought. Pain shot through his head, followed swiftly by his back jarring as the ground flew up to meet him, winding him soundly. He tasted blood, profuse from his ruptured lip, covering his chin and flowing down on to his shirt front. He looked up through eyes blurred and heavy with tears, to see the carpenter being restrained. He was too stunned to think straight, not wishing to know why he had been assaulted. He dabbed his fingers at his mouth, then held them up so that he could see the damage more clearly. He laughed out loud at the absurd thought that it was a beautiful shade of red, as he turned his hand this way and that to catch the light. Then his eyes began to ache with the close focus and he looked beyond to the faces bathed in orange light, turned towards him, expectant.

'I'm sorry . . . I'm so sorry,' he stammered, lowering his gaze to somewhere near waist height.

Everyone was quiet, instinctively deferring to Lord Palmer to take control. He did so with the restraint of a man who has nothing to prove, with no need to posture or shout. He apologised first to Michael, offering a hand to raise him from the ground before inviting him to go home and clean himself up. When he had gone, he turned to Jack, released now but still bristling from the confrontation, his shoulders held in defiance, his feet set in obstinacy. Lord Palmer held his eyes for what seemed like endless minutes before Jack softened, lowering his head and offering an apology.

'No, Jack. Stay,' Lord Palmer was saying in a tone which was not an invitation. Then, more generally, 'Carry on. Forget the trouble. Tomorrow will be a better day for it.'

The fiddle played again and although the notes were the same, the mood took time to return. Spirits revived, the younger ones and drunker ones especially managing to forget themselves, celebrating the present.

15

The day started with thunder, strange in the early morning, then a shower of rain which fizzed and steamed from the ash and embers of the main fire. In the wider fields the animals stood huddled with backs arched and their feet tucked under them, grouping in the lee of hedgerows and under the canopies of the trees in an attempt to stay dry. Across the estate, dogs could be heard barking and singing, tortured by the air rupturing above them. Pheasants called in the woods, and out in the yard the cockerel crowed for the second time.

He poured his coffee and stirred without thinking, his mind preoccupied with the ordeal of the morning – giving her ladyship the garden tour. He liked her very much and this annual examination was the only source of tension between them, a reaffirmation of the hierarchy, an exposure of the true situation which for the rest of the year was ignored. She had smiled wickedly at him over the brim of her glass the night before and when finally the ebb and flow of the others had brought them together, she had been her usual seductive self, emphasising her words with a hand upon his arm, long pauses, and a rich contralto. They had talked about galleries visited and exhibitions seen, the changes in Africa, and the forests of Poland. Everything and nothing, but when he had made his excuses, thinking he could still make bed by two, she had leaned in close to him, her face bathed in orange, enigmatic in the flickering light of the fire, and her tone serious, 'We will talk tomorrow,' before turning away and seeking the side of her husband. It was only to be expected.

He walked to the Hall so that he would have some exercise in the course of the day, the dogs lighter in mood now that the

storm had passed, running madly or stopping to roll themselves in the long wet grass, picking up ticks which he would
have to remove later. The drive was the pale spine of a huge
beast, the cinder marks where ribs had been, the neck twisting away over the field and terminating in a monstrous head,
a sigh of pale, thin smoke rising there still. He kennelled
them, stopping to stroke Simon's pair before passing on to the
Hall.

The door was ajar and he stepped through on to the patterned stone, smiling as the fragrance of lilies greeted him;
life had returned to the Hall. Jack was there, as was Simon,
though they stood at opposite sides of the hallway like
naughty children and were not speaking. He said his 'Good
morning' and seated himself in one of the chairs by the fireplace, considering the carving of the mantel, the fine detail of
the acanthus leaves the stonemason had achieved, bringing a
lightness to the marble, a translucence. In time there was a
shuffling of feet behind him as Simon and Jack adjusted their
weight but they were a long way away and the warm hands
upon his shoulders caught him by surprise.

'There, I thought you were dreaming.' Lady Palmer was
looking down at him kindly. 'I've been out once already. It's
as beautiful as ever . . . I don't know how you've had the
time.'

He held the door for her but she stopped on the threshold
looking back.

'For goodness' sake sit down, the pair of you. You look like
a couple of stuffed animals. Ghastly. It'll be half an hour at
least.'

He suppressed a smile at their awkwardness, so uncharacteristic, and at their relief when they realised it was not
required. Once outside, she slipped her arm through his and
the serious business of a garden tour began.

They walked for two hours, stopping if she showed particular
interest in something or if she thought that she ought to, and

to cut any flowers which took her fancy. Their progress was like that of two shy lovers, as he presented her with bloom after bloom and she bent her head to smell them, signalling acceptance, a deeper tranquillity settling in her eyes as the journey of the day before receded and the time of rest in the green peace of home began. Only once did they have to seek shelter from a shower, finding cover in the corner of a high wall where a wisteria, growing vigorously on the other side, had arced over, spreading out a leafy pavilion. The last of the blossom lay at their feet, mingling with the fine gravel, softening it and dampening its sound.

She had not approached the subject he was expecting and he thought perhaps she was waiting for him to mention it, to gauge from his telling, unconditioned by her questions, the truth of his report. Though the weight of it grew with each passing step, the pressure of it building until it was becoming compelling, he resisted, not out of fear but simply because he had nothing to say, or perhaps no order in which to say it. He was caught off guard when she asked about fencing.

'What, the entire estate?'

'The peninsula should suffice,' she answered.

'Double-fenced, you say? Why? The woods have always been sufficient to discourage visitors.' He was astonished; the calculation of the expense occupied half his mind, the other half running on in speculation.

'It's not about keeping out, but keeping something in.' She paused for effect, enjoying his bemusement. 'Wolves.'

'Wolves.' It was the sigh of a dream which answered her, and although he was looking straight at her he was seeing the only wolf he had ever seen, myopic with cataracts, incarcerated on that concrete island, untamed by age. The sorrow he felt at the memory and the euphoria at the thought of seeing them run free, played across his face.

'Do you think people would accept them? And accept a fence?'

'Hmm.' He tried to marshal his thoughts into some order, his hand seeking out his pocket, empty of supplies. 'The fence is another step, isn't it?' He was hesitant, finding his words. 'I don't think you would hear any objections but without trying it I don't think you will discover the effects it might have either. Some might find it too much.'

'And the wolves?'

'You knew I would love the idea, how can I give you a fair answer?' He shook his head at her, his eyes ablaze with the excitement of it.

'Well, do try,' she persisted.

'I think you could win the argument logically. Emotionally? Are we mature enough as a community? I think so.'

'I had thought so too.' Her words were carefully measured and he sensed the danger of the approaching subject and sought to delay it.

'The shooting would stop, I assume.'

'Inevitably.'

'Do you mind me asking what prompted it?'

'Tiredness, really.' Her voice was heavy and dulled with sadness. She retrieved a box of cigarettes from her pocket, offering him one and surprised when he declined. 'Yes, fatigue, world-fatigue. We stayed away for so long to see how we felt. There seems to be more sorrow, more cruelty, more violence – all these bombs everywhere. It seems to have grown and, well . . .'

'Yes, but why now? Why wolves?' He was urgent, needing to know.

'They sell the stalking rights, not to control the population but to generate hard currency. They shoot more than are needed so the population is in decline. This dying for plea-sure, well, it just seems symptomatic. The commercial shoots will stop whether or not we get the licence. We can-not change the wider world but this place is ours. It can be a haven.'

They looked hard at one another, the recent events

acknowledged between them. She saved him from his conflict with a hand upon his arm.

'You acted well. Even if it turns out to have been one of us, then the punishment has been seen and I doubt the crime will be repeated. What did you use?'

'*Atropa belladonna*, in tincture,' he replied, his voice flat.

'Oh! Nasty.' She winced as she said it. 'And risky.'

'It seemed . . . appropriate.'

She stroked his cheek and kissed him. 'Does it trouble you that he might be innocent?' she asked, searchingly.

'Not especially. Besides, I thought it was the extent of his guilt which remained to be known. And even that, well . . . you've seen her?'

'Of course.'

'I don't know.' There was despair in his voice. 'I guessed it would be one way to protect him from other harm until your return. If he could be seen to suffer.'

She nodded and relinked arms, signalling the progress to continue, saying no more about it for the present. When they parted she had one more question for him.

'Do you think much about the future?'

'My own or the estate's?' He was uncertain, caught off guard again by a tangent.

'You see a difference. Your own, then.'

'I try not to.'

'No . . . no. We must talk of that at some point.'

* * *

Jack sought him out in the afternoon, finding him cleaning the mowers from the day before.

'I just thought I'd come to apologise,' he began without hesitation.

'What for?' He set down his rag and straightened up.

'Y' know. For laying the bastard flat.'

'Ah well, it's done now. Would you like a tea?'

'Aye. A quick one.' They moved through to the bothy,

170

settling at the long table. 'The lads away?'

'Hmm. Adam's out riding with Suzie. I don't know what the others are up to.'

'I cracked his tooth, apparently.'

He nodded but made no other response, setting down two mugs on the table and succumbing to his first roll-up of the day, tempted by the smell of Jack's pipe.

'Was it difficult, this morning?'

'Well. It could have been worse. I'm on my way round to apologise, I just thought I'd do you first.'

'The lesser of two evils, eh?' His smile lupine as he said it.

'The greater, most probably, but an honest one.' His eyes were sparkling with mischief himself.

'Has he been seen today?'

'Yes, he's been in at the Hall all afternoon, shut up in the study. I'm to wait for him there.'

They lapsed into a silence which was broken by a knock upon the door jamb from a tanned and smiling Lucia. Jack flushed and coughed and stumbled to his feet, stammering excuses.

'Don't go for my sake,' Lucia consoled him.

'No, I was on my way somewhere anyway.' He shot his friend a look, 'Thanks for the tea,' and was gone.

Lucia flattened herself to let him past but did not leave her station.

'So, are you going to welcome me back?' she asked coyly.

'Welcome back.' He did not move from the bench, the anticipation of the telling didn't thrill him.

'Oh, please. You can do better than that.'

It was to be a day for words, by all appearances, and his morale sank despite the pleasure he had in seeing her. The time away had done her good and she seemed well settled in herself. The simplicity of her tailored white shirt flattered her figure and her face and was rescued from puritanism by the generous silver and turquoise necklace which she sported in such a way that it must be new. They kissed in the middle of the floor, her lips softly sensuous, pressing into him. She bit his bottom lip as he went to pull away, before breaking off and laughing mischievously.

'What happened to your mouth?' She traced the scab with her finger.

'An act of love . . . Shall we walk?' he asked, hoping it would please her.

'You could show me the cloister again.' She was leading, teasing, re-establishing herself in his life.

'I could. But the moon pond is more relaxing at this time of day.'

They walked arm in arm and he thought it strange that he should spend his day as a husband to other men's wives. She seemed unconcerned about being seen by Michael, leaning into him when they stopped, resting her head upon his shoulder, or reaching up to kiss him again, seriously and more seriously, the playfulness left behind. The woods were cool and humid and she leaned closer still, sharing his warmth until he succumbed, and laying his arm across her shoulders, she clasped his waist.

In the glade of the pool the air was still. The sky above, framed so perfectly by the circles of trees in full leaf, was a clear, pale blue, reflecting in the mirrored surface of the water. He could hear her breathing growing deeper beside him, like repeated sighs, as she explored thoughts of her own. They rested for a while, just standing, listening to the few birds which had not yet gone out of song, and absorbing the mood. When he thought their silence might become terminal, he took her hand and led her to the water's edge. They leaned out over it, as far as they could, trying to fill their vision with the sky below them without their faces appearing in the water. They laughed at their game and it was easy between them.

Slowly he turned, smoothing her hair back from her face and tucking it behind her ear. She kissed the inside of his wrist as he did so and he thrilled to the touch of it.

'Not yet,' he whispered, a frown puckering her forehead briefly before the smile returned. He unbuttoned her shirt and eased it from her shoulders, holding it for her as she drew her arms out from the sleeves. He unfastened her bra and she surrendered that too, their eyes locked together throughout. He undressed her fully, resisting the urge to kiss those arms, the top of her thigh, the hollow of her knee, laying the clothes aside neatly at the base of a tree. She in turn undressed him, succumbing only once, kissing the muscle of his shoulder as she slid the shirt from his back.

At the water's edge they turned and smiled a smile of deep appreciation before turning back and, as one, diving into the pool, passing beneath the surface and throwing up gentle ripples. It was warm from the day, warmer than the air, and they swam together, kissing and parting, diving down or floating as the mood took them.

They lay together on the grass until they were dry and starting to chill, reluctantly dressing again, feeling the clothes awkward and rough against their skin. They were returning to the mundane.

'Where's your car?' he asked, wondering if Michael knew yet.

'Behind the stable block. Why?'

'Good. I need to collect the dogs. Then we can go home.'

* * *

He lit the fire when they reached his cottage, as much for the comfort as the warmth. She slipped off her shoes and curled up on the settee, watching him observe the rituals of hearth sweeping, paper twisting, and the stacking of kindling. She was enjoying his movements, the way in which he could be there with her, then away, absorbed by his work, his hands so fluid in action. When it was done, the flames beginning to dance, throwing shadows up around his face, he turned and kissed her, not rising from his knees, and turned back to the fire to be sure. When he was satisfied with its progress he left

173

it, going out to the kitchen. She heard the pop of a cork and the faintest chink of glasses, and stretched out her arms in satisfaction.

He sat on the floor with his back against the settee and they talked their way through the first bottle. She had arranged herself an exhibition, fairly low-key as befitted her ambition. The work was primarily to keep herself amused and he felt as she talked that the event was more of the same – a focus, voluntary and somewhat artificial, but a useful exercise for her ingenuity.

They ate a light supper of salad, fresh bread, and cheese, picnicking in front of the fire as inertia gripped them. Time became hazy, the slowly fading evening apparently endless, the bells of the hall clock somehow lost to them. The words were out almost before he realised but he did not retract them – he wanted her there when he slept and when he woke. Despite her inebriation, her wits remained sharp.

'On one condition,' she pounced.

'Yes?' He waited but he half-expected what it would be.

'Let me photograph you.' Her eyes were sparkling as if this was the endgame she had been playing for.

'Why do you wish to so much?' He had been surprised by her persistence all along. She leaned in close to him so that her breath was hot against his ear, whispering her answer conspiratorially as if there were many there who might hear. She drew back again, sipping her wine and affirming the challenge with a raise of her eyebrows. It was not the reason he had been expecting.

'On one condition,' he replied.

'Yes?' She too could play coy.

'Don't show my face.'

'It won't steal your soul, you know.' Her irritation was disguised as mockery.

'No, indeed. How could it? How could it?' She was struck by the meditative fall of those last words and knew that she was approaching something to be handled with care. She

174

planned her shoot, looking over the top of his head and staring into the fire, considering the possibilities. He stared into the flames too but was no longer thinking, only waiting until it was time to welcome sleep.

She set up against the blank wall of the unused bedroom, the porous distemper an accommodating background for the effect she wished to create. He came through from the bath, his hair still wet and glistening, pale beads falling on to his shoulders and chest as he walked. He was very far away and had she wished to take his face surreptitiously, she would have been unable, as his eyes looked straight through her as if she was not there. She consoled herself with the breakthrough of his agreement; the difficulty of the process would only serve to sweeten the end result. They worked in half-hour bursts followed by a break. In the first one he returned with coffee and stood at the open window looking out, smoking. He was better in the second session, as if he had come to some resolution in the interim.

She worked her way through her mental catalogue and he was intrigued by the details which had caught her attention; things about himself that he would not have given any thought to. She double-exposed every frame, the first take more in focus than the second, overlaying a hard image with one which blurred the boundaries. She would tint them differently, mostly with different pale blues, colours of the skies she had seen here. One she over-washed with red. The final prints had a spectral aura, the figure emerging from the soft wall, a figure emerging from the figure. His eyes had softened and were more focused upon her as she viewed them through the camera. She resisted the urge to take them, though, steeped as they were in a sadness she could not fathom. Some of the pictures she desired would make more sense with a face, but she knew she had reached the threshold of what could be sustained between them. He was allowing her to see this, so typical of him – to do this now when she could not ask the questions that the looks he gave her prompted. His attitude to images was peculiar. She was desperate to check the drawer to see the cliff-top again, now that she shared the experience with the unknown photographer. Now that the picture of Anna had gone from beside the bed. She had seen him observe her surprise but he had not volunteered information and she had not wished to ask just then. She was glad, if anything, to be free of those dark eyes in that beautiful face, to be free of the challenge and the judgement of her predecessor.

The early afternoon brought it to a close. He had achieved a boredom so deep-seated now as to negate the benefits of perseverance. He watched her from the step as she walked back towards the Hall, before setting off for a long walk with the dogs; his limbs ached with inactivity and the tension of the withheld confession.

Michael was up at the Hall, struggling under the scrutinising gaze of Lord Palmer, feeling much more like the subject than the artist. Lucia was pleased to be coming into an empty house, to have time to unpack her things and get settled without interference and questions. She wandered around with no fixed purpose, sorting one thing before moving on to another in no particular order. She was pleased by the evidence of work in her absence and impressed by some of the pictures. The market might have turned sufficiently for some of them to make some serious money. She was less pleased by the stack of empty bottles she found secreted in the rear porch as if she might not find them there. His capacity seemed to be increasing all the time. She was puzzled by the noises she could hear from upstairs and thought a bird must have got in through an open window. She went up to investigate, pausing on the landing and cocking her head to pinpoint the source. She sighed as she recognised the sound of rats running in the roof space, a sound which prompted an unexpected nostalgia for her childhood home. It was an unusual time of year to get them in and despite the nostalgia she would mention it and have them removed. She really could not stand the creatures.

She frowned when she saw the paper on the floor in the doorway, shaking her head and feeling impatient with her husband. She stooped to pick it up, instinctively turning it over to see what was on the reverse. The face was upside down and its hideousness not fully apparent until she rotated it. She was shocked; the depiction of horror was really very good, one of the best drawings of Michael's she had seen. She restored it to the desk, finding others and stacking them, flicking at them appreciatively and wondering at their motivation. The laughing head like a gargoyle particularly took her fancy and she placed it on top of the pile. She turned away, glancing towards the picture which lay against the wall behind the door. At a distance it seemed quite innocuous, but the quality was such that it drew her over and she crouched down to examine it closer. She reeled at the sickness of it, her mouth twisting in an expression which was not a smile. If it was a true reflection of his erotic ideal then she wanted no part of it. She would not play those games or be thought of in that way, not knowingly or willingly.

16

The gardener's cottage was a vanity here at the far end of the estate, for the drive that ran to it and through the wrought-iron gates led nowhere. Beyond the walls it travelled fifty yards, turning across a pretty stone bridge which arced over a stream, then nothing. The gravel had never even been laid and the only track that pushed through the grass and shrubby under-storey at the edge of the woods was made by deer, who found the bridge a useful addition to their world, saving them the scramble down and up the banks to the lush grazing beneath the demesne wall.

The large key lived on a hook behind his door and he reached for it now and headed out, the dogs at heel. The lock had other ideas, though, and despite his strength, he could not turn it, realising now that he had not been out this way since the autumn of the year before. He rested his head against the bars for a minute, but they had not been designed for comfort and he trudged back to the lodge for a different sort of key, bidding the dogs stay. One sharp blow of the mash on the cold chisel was enough to separate the skin of rust, and the key turned stiffly now. He made a note to himself to not be so neglectful of his duties as a lodge-keeper and to oil it properly before much more time had passed. Dragging the gate open through the long grass, just far enough for him to pass through sideways, he went out.

He cut up the deer track into the woods, the dogs running on, their noses fixed to the earth, their muscles tense with whatever exotic excitements this never-used track promised. Fat pigeons struggled up from the ground with straining hearts as they approached; rabbits scattering into bramble thickets; the high-pitched yelps of the chase all that followed them. Step by step his heart eased and his mind approached peace, saturated by the smells and sounds of the wood which barely recorded his passing. He was unhurried, meandering along the tracks of least resistance so long as they were mostly upwards. He knew that even at this pace within an hour the trees would thin and the grass give way to bilberry and heather, some scrubby oak and birch, then, if he went high enough, moorland proper with cotton grass marking the raised bogs.

He felt strong at the woodland edge and pressed on, relishing the gusting wind, cold and full of salt. He had a perverse desire to view the estate and climbed on towards the crags from where he could overlook the woods. Phlebus and Sally were springing over heather clumps, raising grouse they would never catch, and it was difficult not to smile at the tails waving like flags as they coursed the ground.

The wind blew faster and stronger at the summit, carrying spits of moisture which stung his face. He sat down at the top and swung his legs out over the edge, taking in his world. The clouds across the valley cast black shadows on the land and he knew he did not have long before the storm reached him. White slashes on the surface of the lough spoke of waves and even the spires of smoke from the more sheltered cottages were skewed away from the chimneys and broken. He could see horses, though, running in the paddock, and a splash of colour here and there indicated a body going about. The Hall itself was hidden by its trees and the angle to his own cottage was too acute from here. Inevitably his eyes came to rest on the Dower but he closed them, wishing Michael and Lucia away. But for the wind in his ears and the panting of the dogs, all was quiet.

He turned his head without seeing until his eyes came to the edges of the world that lay beyond his; their world, Anna's world. What was it Anna had written in her last letter? – that he would never be free of himself – and his angered response, short and to the point, that he should not have posted. Since then no word and he did not blame her. Perhaps this way she could be free of him finally, and free of any regret for a life which could never have been. Perhaps this way it was better.

He leaned forward over the edge, looking past his feet to the ground below, where rocks split from this escarpment by frost lay tumbled among the heather. He was never sure of heights but reckoned it forty feet at most. He barely had to move to find out if it were enough, another inch forward and his weight would take him. Sally nudged at his elbow and he straightened, putting an arm around her neck for comfort.

'There's you two to think of, of course.' Phlebus shuffled forward at his voice, pressing against his thigh. Despite their warmth, he shivered. 'Although that could be solved.' Sally's almond eyes were almost level with his own and he looked into them, past the growing cloud of cataract, seeing the trust. He ran his fingers through the coat at her neck and she stretched out her chin with appreciation. Over her throat they moved, up and down, picking out the artery between thumb and forefinger, her body becoming still beneath his hand. He shifted his weight and slowly removed his knife from his hip pocket where Phlebus was lying against it making it sore. He laid it on the ledge behind him and stroked them both. 'Funny,' he spoke again to them, 'it would be easier to cast you adrift down there than to settle the issue. Which would you choose, given the choice?'

There was the finding, of course. He had left that gate open, stupidly, and they would be bound to look up here. 'You'd be burnt as a witch, Phlebus Samsdogger.' He wiped a hand across dry eyes; it would almost be worth it to be free of the horror of that day. To be free of himself at last, perhaps. His tongue probed the scab on his lip absently. It was the sounds that had stayed with him. His hand was on the gate when first he heard, his heart quickening as his body understood and responded, his mind crawling along behind trying to make sense of the animal screams. The door was stood open, then the kitchen. On the table, Magda, her leg bared, luminous in the evening light, bent at the knee and curled around him as if in love. He'd pinned her hands above her head; he was strong still. She looked like a child beside him. A bottle of wine was on its side and two glasses half-filled, the liquid swilling about with the movement of the table so that it splashed out. He could not take his eyes off those glasses, the yellow wine catching the light, over and over. Magda got her head turned towards him, her face red with blood from smashing Sam's nose, she was screaming his name now and he was able to move again, catching Sam off balance as he tried to free himself, gathering Magda up and putting the table between them and him. Sam panting, wild-eyed, across from them, priapic still.

'She wanted it.' Uncertain, the edge of madness to his voice. Again, 'She wanted it!' More determined now, making it true despite the blood which flowed from nose and ears.

'Leave Sam.' His voice strangled and strange to himself. He was out with Magda, into the air, into the parkland, though the grass was long and wet, and Magda sobbed behind him as he dragged her by the wrist. A single, muffled shot stopped them, Magda dropping into the meadow. He looked down at her, surprised she had understood, then back towards the Dower where the jackdaws were settling back upon their nest on the far chimney. He cleaned her face and hands with a switch of wet grass, as much as she would let him. Finally, he got her raised and they walked unhurriedly to the Hall. The lies he would tell could wait; nobody would contest them. Let Sam be mourned properly, for the life he had lived until this final complication. He regretted this perverse compassion for the dead which had let the living suffer. Elsie had been right, but what of it? It was too late to change the history of that time.

The first squall hit him hard and he looked up stunned. The lough and half the park were gone. A fresh spire of smoke was billowing from near the trees. Wondering who had lit his hearth, he raised himself, the dogs following, stretching out and shaking before springing away on the hunt again.

He found a salad on the table and potatoes simmering on the hob. He was just checking the oven when Lucia appeared.

'Mint for the spuds,' she said by way of explanation, and slipped by him to the sink to rinse it.

'Trout?'

'Yes, they were on the table. I cleaned and gutted them and everything. Aren't I clever?' She leaned beyond him to pop the mint into the pan and kissed him on the cheek as she did so.

'I'll open some wine,' he said to cover his bemusement and wandered to the pantry. He fetched two glasses and poured, handing one to Lucia who had perched herself on the table's edge. As he came within range she drew him in with a bare heel; she was wearing one of his shirts again.

'I called and called for you. Where were you?'

'Walking.' And he gestured with his head in the direction of the gate. At her frown he explained, 'I don't go that way very often.'

'You're soaked. You should take these off.' And she began unbuckling his belt for him. Sensing his reluctance, she was all seduction. 'We've time.'

'Later, lass. I'll go and change.' Her lip was out so he kissed it, then gulped some wine, removing himself from her embrace and away.

* * *

It would prove a strange month for Inchnamactaire. Michael endured sessions with Lord Palmer, growing more ragged and frayed as his nerves grew stretched under the unwavering eye. It was not even hostility, just an intensity of concentration he had never encountered in a sitter. He would mix his palette with tentative hands, invariably too little, feeling he was taking too long over it. He sipped water constantly, wetting dry lips with his tongue. The click of the glass as he set it down was enough to put his nerves on edge; the pendulum of the clock a constant irritation he could not ignore. His eyes would dart towards it several times an hour, watching the slow crawl of time. Then Lord Palmer would speak, a question that had to be answered, and he would try, hesitant and flustered, but he could not shake off the feeling he had not understood and would replay it in his mind, expanding his response, changing it until he thought he knew what was wanted, over and over. He felt like a prisoner and his resentment towards his patron grew and blossomed into a strange flower.

His favourite time of day became the few short minutes at the end of a session. Lord Palmer would thank him and leave the room, and he could pack his things methodically, putting them in order. The portrait could stay in place – the room was not being used for anything else – and he would turn the key in the lock behind him and turn out over the park towards the Dower. The walk would bring some quiet to his mind. The land here had a permanence, a settledness that seemed to emit strength. He would stop and listen to the absence of mechanical noise, watching the movement of the wind over the grass, a caressing hand bending the stems as it passed. The leaves at play on the trees. Some days he wanted to lie down in the sward, feeling the earth beneath his back, the sky framed by the nodding grass, and just cease. No more clocks. It was a peace that passed his understanding. Other times it made him want to scream, just to hear a human sound within it. He could feel himself suffocating, his eyes becoming blinkered and myopic, as he strained to shut out this ever-shifting life. Either way, the point would come, sooner or later, when the thought of the Dower could not be avoided.

It was a twisted little roulette Lucia had been playing. There were the days she had not been there at all and others when she had been in – things had been moved, tidied. Anxiously, he would set down his bags and go straight up the stairs, dragging the chair over to the wardrobe and examining his icon on the top of it for signs of disturbance. He would eat early, heating the food which was being provided for him now and which he had accepted without question, the silent acknowledgement of his humiliation, and open a bottle of wine. He was finding some comfort in the simple duty of washing and drying his dishes. It seemed to put a completeness on his day. Lucia had brought him cigarettes. At first they had made him nauseous but gradually he had recovered his taste for them. Taking one outside with a glass of wine, he strolled about the garden and ticked off another day. Steadily, this time will pass, he consoled himself, and then we'll see. An hour could be lost in the bath if he tried really hard, then he would shave, staring at the hollows in his cheeks and pulling the loose skin of his neck taut for the razor. His hair was becoming duller and thinning at the temples. He combed it through, gathering up the lost ones and comparing their number to the day before. Each morning there seemed to be more on his pillow and he wondered how there could be any left on his head at all. The rest of his evening he spent looking. He obsessed over his own image in the mirror, poring over the familiar detail which somehow seemed not to belong to him any more. The man behind the eyes had a very curious look. Eventually, tiring of this, he would take down his Magda, placing it on the window-sill where the light would catch it aslant. His drinking was steady and in time a smile formed upon his face as he remembered happier days.

Sometimes, without explanation, Lucia was there and they ate together, talking like strangers about his work and how best to arrange the final viewing here and who best to speak to when back in London. She would photograph them for the catalogue and they talked through ideas for the text. The unspoken hung above them like stale cigarette smoke, settling in a pall until they wanted air. At times he thought there might be tenderness in her words, she was very encouraging

184

about the pictures, but it was just the twist of the knife, he decided. A chaste kiss on the cheek and she would take herself upstairs to bed, shutting the bedroom door with a determined click. He uncorked more wine and drank without pleasure, her silence a brooding presence in the house. Her presence an obstacle to looking at his Magda. In the mornings she was gone, when he awoke dressed but cold on the couch in his studio, thinking of other couches and other studios and the pleasures he had taken there. He collected up some drawings from the desk and sat before the hearth. He balled one and lit it, watching the flame spread, the paper opening out in the heat. When it was nearly out he placed another flat upon it until it too caught. One by one, he worked his way through the faces and forms he had drawn in that frenzied time of Lucia's absence, feeling warmer now than when he woke.

A knocking at the door drew his attention away from the smoking, charred paper. Jack was waiting there and instinctively Michael drew back in fear, his hand rising to protect his mouth.

'I've come to measure up for packing cases,' Jack said, the pipe clamped firmly in his teeth.

'Right . . . Come in. They're mostly down the passage in the end room.' He pointed, standing well clear as Jack stepped forward. The pipe smoke made him gag. 'Would you mind putting that out?' He shifted his weight nervously as he spoke, his hand at his face all the while.

'Makes no difference to me.' Jack tapped it on the door jamb, dislodging the contents on to the path before returning it empty to his lips.

Michael was very wary but Jack seemed helpful, asking questions about preferences and demonstrating a good knowledge of just what was required; not losing patience even though Michael kept having to ask him to repeat, struggling with the obscuring pipe. Jack's attention kept wandering to the fireplace.

'Just some drawings I didn't want to keep,' Michael felt obliged to explain, perturbed by the steady gaze Jack turned upon him, his eyes of grey and brown inscrutable.

He was relieved finally to get Jack out of the house and retreated upstairs to watch from a window as he shambled off, stopping at the gate to spit and relight, an eye on the house all the while he was doing so. Michael drew back so as not to be seen, shaking his head. Freaks, failures and fools, that's all they were here and the sooner he and Lucia were away, the better. Perhaps in London they could start afresh, putting this madness behind them. He was beyond jealousy over the situation. There was just a dullness, a numbness of his mind which left him enervated and drawn. There was not long to go, that was his true comfort, though its approach was slow. He just had to hold on. As much a question of nerve as strength, and easier now that he had been released from painting Amelia, accepting the reason given without question. He never suspected they might know he had already fulfilled that part of the arrangement if only for his own private satisfaction.

* * *

Lucia was distracted as she crossed the demesne; ten more days at most, Michael had reckoned, then her excuse for remaining here would have been exhausted. Decisions needed to be made before then and, despite her manner, she preferred to breeze along than have to make any. She avoided thinking by admiring the beautiful land, quite lush finally, down here in the shelter of the trees. The trees themselves were many and varied and the mosaic of their foliage reminded her of the north window of her local church, all shades of green in an abstract pattern, a virtue that had saved them from Cromwell's iconoclasts. She toyed with taking a few shots but really could not be bothered any more. All that she had wanted she had had, save one or two minor irritations. She had been amazed by Michael's fascination with them. As far as she was concerned, a tree was a tree was a tree, and she did not anticipate having particular memories of these ones. The hills were a different proposition, now – the way the distance seemed to change so that one day they would appear to be sat glowering over the Hall and the next they would be far off, aloof like some angry old god. Or serene perhaps; it was difficult to pin down. She imagined that was why Michael had avoided the attempt, though he had never confessed as much. For that, at least, she did not reproach him. She knew, as she looked at the hills now, that below her, her lover would be looking too as he did so often, his eyes slipping focus and wandering there in unattended moments, so that she would have to bring him back with a word or a nudge. It was as if he was always waiting for something. She had asked him why, just the once, and he had smiled slightly and lowered his eyes to the ground, mumbling an answer which she had not really heard. She knew by his manner that it would not be repeated and she had let it go, like so much else. He seemed to have developed layers until at last he was like a pearl with a hard, polished surface. The world could wash over and around him but it would not stick. A surface which changed colour as it moved beneath the light until it defied classification. She had been happy with this image and had shared it with Lady Palmer when they bumped into each other in the pretty little walled garden, now sadly past its best. Drifts of browned blossom lay against the bases of walls and the irises held up the bleached and withered standards of faded glory. Work had begun to remove them, as the half-filled barrow testified, but the worker had been sent elsewhere, leaving them free to talk. She remembered the swelling buds as she had last seen the place, less troubled then than now. The proportion was still pleasing, though, and seasoned her memories, making them palatable. The air was quiet, with the to-ing and fro-ing of bumble bees, the only life.

'I like the idea of layers,' Lady Palmer had replied, 'but isn't a pearl too mineral? More like a tree perhaps, adding a ring with each passing year.'

187

There was silence for a moment whilst Lady Palmer lit a cigarette and waved a hand at a cloud of midges that had discovered them. 'You know, some trees become hollow as they grow older. Oaks do it. And yews. It seems to make them stronger.'

'So an old tree is mostly dead?' Lucia had asked, surprised.

'No, what remains is as alive as ever. There's just a lot missing.'

They had left it at that and talked for some time of other things. She had been glad to have made their acquaintance, generous hearted and easy in a manner which seemed to be growing rarer in her world. When she had stood to leave, there had been one more surprise.

'Lucia . . . dear . . . it would be a mistake to fall in love with him.'

She had had no intention of falling in love with him, but as she caught sight of him in the distance, standing on a slight rise, all legs and shoulders, his head turned out towards the hill as anticipated, she was not so sure of herself. He turned at her approach, despite her attempts to surprise him. The gentleness of his smile had been restored by his time alone and she felt a twinge of hurt. Worse still were his quiet words of greeting and the faintest touch of his hand upon her back as he kissed her, all invitations to which her traitor body responded.

'I thought we should ride out today. I've horses saddled and ready.'

She took the roan and settled herself, feeling her muscles relax into the so-familiar posture. They were well schooled and responsive and she enjoyed the challenge of having to ride properly, knowing that her mare would not compensate for mixed signals with inertia. His grey was a similar stand but fuller in the girth and heavier in the shoulders and haunches. The thickness of the neck was accentuated by the hogged mane, a darkening ridge of bristles. They warmed up slowly before trotting, covering the distance swiftly, the mounts eager. He led them down towards the shore of the lough, picking their way carefully along a narrow track, the undergrowth high around them, brushing their legs and catching between their feet and the stirrups. She recognised the vista from the strand, the low island with its skeleton trees, and looked at him sharply to see if it was a deliberate choice. He was swinging from the saddle, landing with a light crunch on the shingle, and saying over the prow that both horses liked the water. She dismounted too and they unbuckled the girths, laying the saddles aside with their shoes. He helped her back up, cradling her bare foot in his hands as he hoisted her. They were happy in the water, cooling off from the heat of the day and finding some relief from the flies which had risen from the bracken and pursued them.

When they reached the island they let the horses graze and returned to the lough, enjoying the rise and fall of the few waves which textured its surface. They talked disconnectedly as they swam, as if they did not believe in it but the habit of conversation could not be broken. They lingered there, delaying the moment of getting out. Like stopping smoking, he thought as he watched her face above the water, his body would have to relearn patterns when she was gone. Strange how one life moulds to another.

17

The note on his table had been written with a precision he could not fault. There were no spare words. He took it in at a glance, then looked over the envelope to Lucia who was standing, smelling the honeysuckle that had been placed upon the table and trying hard not to show her curiosity. He turned from her, lifted the latch of the range door and posted the note into the fire.

'Love letters?' she failed.

'No. Just a request from his lordship. Something he wants doing sooner rather than later.'

He filled a glass and took the blossom from her, placing two of the stems in the water. On a whim, he smoothed her hair back from her face and tucked the third behind her ear, kissing her gently on the forehead.

'You're sending me away, aren't you?'

'Yes.'

She sank on to a chair, an elbow on the table and a hand to the side of her face. He was too close to her to remain standing and moved round, taking a seat across from her.

'Your husband is grinding to a halt. He needs you if he is to finish.'

'That was what the note said?'

'Near enough.'

Her eyes were focusing somewhere near the middle of the table, her hands restlessly lifting and replacing a box of matches. It was painful to watch her beauty breaking down, her cheeks becoming pale and blotched, a nervousness at her mouth. Her breathing slowed to a stop then was broken, as a deep, uneven intake would grip her.

'Could not that girl help him?' Each word was clipped as she struggled with control.

'Magda spends most of her time in her room now. It is better she has the familiar around her until . . . She is taken for walks . . . when your husband is with Lord Palmer, but not out of sight of the Hall. It is better she doesn't see him.'

She looked at him keenly now, the picture of Magda springing vividly to her mind. 'Did he do something?'

'We think so.' He took the matches from her, setting them away beyond her reach.

'And you would send me back to him?'

He looked at her steadily, amazed that even her reaction to this was self-absorbed.

'I could leave him.' Hope crept into her tone.

'It would be different if you stayed. Besides, that is not my . . .'

'No. You could come with me and –' Her voice failed as she studied his face; she resumed chewing her bottom lip.

'Lucia, you're a dear girl, but I can't leave here.' A resignation was settling over him; this would have to be endured for some time.

'Why not? What is there to stop you? Answer me! . . . please . . . What are you afraid of?'

His breath whistled out, sharp between clenched teeth. 'It would be just words . . .'

'Try. I'll try to understand.'

'Perhaps I don't wish you to. Sometimes it is better not to know.'

'Let me decide that.'

'No.'

'You are such a bastard.' Her voice nearly a whisper now.

'That too is part of it, yes. But I've always tried to protect those I love. Even from myself.'

The word silenced her and she stared at him through long moments, the sad eyes in the deeply lined face looking back at her long enough for her to know the truth, before turning away to the window, seeking a way out as so many times before.

They drank a glass of whiskey together before she left,

passing it between them, the taking hand enclosing the giving. They were sat in a west-facing window, watching the evening distil its peace over his small garden, the chickens scratching contentedly under the hedge; the land beyond. Her back rested at his chest, his legs and arms wrapped around her. She was peaceful against this now-familiar warmth, the smell of work and sun which radiated from him, earth notes to the spirit. Unconsciously, she traced the hollow at his knee through his trousers, shivering as he smoothed away the hair from her neck, placing a kiss, hot and dry, upon her neck.

At the door he clasped her to himself, tightly now until she felt they would fuse together, then apart enough to rest foreheads, eyes open but unfocused, filled with the face of the other. Finally she disengaged, smoothing his face with a hand which he took, pressing the palm to his lips.

* * *

The evening would start early in deference to the long journey of the following day. The old, low barn which was no longer used had been cleared and swept, and the paintings arranged over the previous days according to Lucia's word. The free-standing pieces were laid out like an avenue, creating a space through which the tree-covered walls could be glimpsed. Michael had withheld the portrait of Lord Palmer as he wished to unveil it personally before all the assembled staff. He had a certain sense of theatre as he entered and found the room filled already, people milling with glasses in hand, eyeing him and the linen-covered frame he carried. He placed it with great aplomb on the easel reserved for it at the western end of the barn, on a kind of dais that had been mocked up with planks on bricks. The hum of indistinct words sounded remarkably positive and he was surprised to register the same sort of first-night nerves he had experienced in the past. He made for the drinks table, in need of a top-up to steady himself. The liquidity of his eyes recorded the toll of plenty he had enjoyed before venturing out. He stood at the edge and sipped his wine watching those who would not approach him, judge him. Would Lucia manage to arrive before their hosts for once in her life, he wondered. She was firmly ensconced and irritable in the bath when he left the Dower.

The question was answered promptly when she appeared in the doorway with the hosts, her arm draped through Lord Palmer's, who patted her hand and released her to her husband when he saw him. Patronage was hateful, he'd known it all along. It was the waiting for the approval of another, always having to be cautious; he did not regret his rendering of this haughty man who was so good as to give him back his wife. Lucia publicly extended the role of supporting wife which she had returned to in private these last days, decorating his side and nodding at all the right moments. She remained on the right side of patronising in her comments, though he could have endured much more, as he had, willingly, in the past, in return for her physical bolstering, adding her mass and charisma to his, giving him confidence.

The talk-round went quite well, Lord Palmer asking probing questions as to details and technique whilst all the time scanning the works as if assessing not only them but the veracity of the answers also. He was holding himself in the game, although he had little hunger for it. They worked down one side, weaving through the gaps in some elaborate dance, coming close to the portrait so that he wished to unveil it then and have done, before veering off to inspect the other side, the portrait receding, postponed but dominating like a malevolent presence. When they were done and judgement had been passed, really very favourable although with some of the words he hated to hear like 'promising', Lord Palmer turned and indicated the covered portrait.

Michael stepped up beside it and cleared his throat, scanning the faces of those assembled before him and waiting for the last of the stragglers to join the back of the group. He began his spiel about perception and representation, watching the lights dim in the eyes of those who had little interest. Amelia slipped through the door at the back, closing it noiselessly and resting against it as if on guard. Her beauty was luminous, her thick black hair swept around and tumbling in curls over her bare shoulder. She was dressed in the simplest of slip dresses which clung to her curves and rippled with the slightest movement, changing colour as it did so, the dark silver of the satin mutable. Her head was cast back and she stared at him. He shifted feet nervously, faltering now and looking about for a glass of water. She was her sister made perfect. Regaining some composure, he spoke for a while about character and personality, its interaction with others, specifically that of the artist, namely him, smoothing first one hand then the other down the front of his trousers in a futile attempt to dry his palms, and how his intention could be divined from the work. He almost laughed as he enunciated 'divine', noticing the lights switch back on as people discerned the care with which he chose his words now and the unexpected direction in which they were being led. He left that to settle in for a moment or two, sipping again to ease his dry mouth, his breathing erratic as he braced himself for what he was about to do. Finally he turned and whipped off the cover, watching the comic faces of the throng as they saw and smiling at the collective gasp. A silence of expectation settled over the room after the initial shock. Only Michael was smiling still and more nervously now that time drew out and nothing was said. He could feel the sweat starting on his collar and looked to Lucia for reassurance. Almost imperceptibly she shook her head.

He had washed the canvas with red, which showed through where the paint was thinner and paler such as the teeth, bared in what might have been a smile if it had not been in association with the feral eyes. He had used a liberal proportion of green in the skin tones, waxing the flesh and rendering it cold like a corpse. With the light from the top, deep shadows were cast by the brow, nose, and chin – dark planes of uncertainty which unshaped the face.

'It is very good indeed, young man,' Lord Palmer pronounced finally. 'I had no idea I was so ferocious.'

The room exploded with words as Lord and Lady Palmer stepped up to examine it more closely. Michael was flattered by the impact of the painting but unsettled that a man could absorb such an affront so benignly. They started to ask him the same questions about technique, appraising it dispassionately as they had the others. He answered as if in a stupor, gulping down the fresh glass of wine which Lucia had brought for him.

'I was wrong. Very good,' she whispered as she handed it over, trailing her eyes over him as she moved away to allow Lady Palmer closer. He managed a smile and ignored the implied criticism of her question.

'As far as paintings, yes, this is everything. I have all my developmental sketches and work books, of course.' He nodded as he said it as if to make it true and was pleased when she expressed an interest in those too.

Whilst this was going on he became aware of a change in the noise level and looked away from her, out over the room. He could see the people parting down the middle, falling silent as they did so. He caught the face of the gardener looking grim, between the heads of the others, and the edge of something he was holding out in front of himself with arms straight, reverentially almost, like an icon. The colour drained from his face when he realised what it was the gardener was carrying and he reached out to support himself, grasping the easel and finding Lord Palmer's hand steadying him at the elbow in a grip which was firmer than was comfortable. When the picture of Magda reached the front, Lord Palmer turned to him, smiling benignly still.

'Tell me, I am curious. Did you not think this was good enough for display? I think it is excellent, perhaps your best.

You have a talent for the grotesque which I had not anticipated. Or perhaps there was a reason apart from quality?' He gestured with his free hand, somewhat blandly, his tone entirely neutral. 'What intention should we be divining from this?'

Michael looked out over the assembled faces, reddening from the heat of the hostility which radiated at him. Lucia was staring with an expression he could not read and he knew he was alone. Lucia who had betrayed him, thinking to be rid of a picture, knowing he could not protest its loss without admitting its existence. Lucia who felt betrayed, knowing nothing of this parade. He swallowed hard, his chest tightening with the effort of control. He turned back to Lord Palmer, caught between him and his portrait.

'I . . .' he began, falteringly, his mouth hot and dry. Lord Palmer raised his brows expectantly.

'I . . . That's mine!' he managed, changing to the attack, frantically looking about for any sign of support.

He heard the gardener growl through clenched teeth. Michael launched himself at him, grabbing his picture by the top and bottom and wrenching at it impotently, until the frame began to give, twisting and breaking at the corner with a sharp crack. The sky was torn in by an inch.

'Mr Berdyaev!' Lord Palmer commanded, and Michael stopped his tugging but did not relinquish his grip. 'Our contract, as I remember, was for you to paint a portrait of myself and one of my daughter. That picture is mine and it will stay here in Inchnamactaire. You shall leave tomorrow. Take it away.'

Jack and Simon closed in front of him, compelling him backwards until he fell against the dais.

The Palmers were leaving and the people drifted away after them, silent now but troubled still. Lucia leaned back against the wall, feeling it cool and solid through her shirt, a fixed point. Only Amelia remained, standing in the middle of the hall, quite unselfconscious as she watched the crumpled figure, folded in upon itself and starting to rock. Lucia regarded her, unsure she could take any more for one evening. She looked down at Michael, the impatience and anger rising within her at his incessant mantra of 'Mine'. She heard steps and looked up to see that her lover had joined the girl. He too was watching Michael intently, witnessing the start of a collapse which went deep to the heart of Michael's mind. A strange look was upon his face, pity yes, but compassion too. They locked eyes for long moments and it seemed to her that he was waiting for a decision which she did not know how to make. He had rejected her; if he was extending an offer now then it was one her pride would not accept. A low cry from Michael broke their contact and he glanced towards Amelia, speaking too faintly for Lucia to hear. She watched as he took the girl's hand and together they left the hall. She looked back at Michael, whose crying was louder now and more erratic. A coldness settled within her and she knew that for now, she would need her strength.

Postscript

He had not expected to hear from her again, but it appeared she wanted to involve him in her life. Although he was expecting company he read it through for a second time, not really wanting the information but feeling somehow obliged. There was talk of parties, fairly low-key events by necessity, and the relative successes of their respective exhibitions. They seemed to have caught their moment to be the celebrity art couple. Michael was fragile still, but was making slow progress with his weekly sessions. He had not seen the funny side of Lucia's series of tree labels, monochrome against the bark, thinking she was mocking his work. Her thanks again for the sedative he had supplied for the drive home. He smiled at her descriptions; she had a fine turn of phrase. She made no mention of the future. He set the letter down and placed a stone upon it to stop it blowing about, putting it and Lucia and Michael from his mind. He rolled his cigarette, moistening his tongue with a sip of whiskey. He leaned back against the door post, turning up his collar to keep out the chill of the night air and stretching out his legs, prompting a grumble from Phlebus. The first of the stars was bright over the hedge. The nights were drawing in.

Acknowledgements

My thanks to my wife Elaine for the listening and the loving. My readers: Sarah and James. My friends, whose comments encouraged: Mireille, Mark, Carol, Jon, Anna,Tom, Lindsey, and Peter, for the thank yous. Valerie for the botanicals and Alan for a roof over our heads. Albert, a prince of men. Pete for the contact and my agent, Kevin. And everybody at Faber and Faber, especially Lee Brackstone and Walter Donohue.